Critters, Hidden Gold, Mayhem,

And
OTHER ODD TALES

By

Fredda J. Burton

Also By Fredda J. Burton

Fiction
The Chocolate Set: A Swedish Journey
From Ellis Island to the Last Best West
Way Too Many Goodbyes
War And Storm
Fleeting As Sunset
Bridges, Beds, and Other Important Things

Non Fiction
Only the Destination Was Wrong:
Hanson-Persson Family History

Numerous Articles and Illustrations
In
Mother Earth News
Countryside Magazine
Tidepools
Outdoor Illinois Magazine
Various Scientific Books and Journals such as:
Forest Trees of Illinois
American Fern Journal
Illinois and Regional Plant Guides
Flora of Illinois

Introduction

This book consists of a series of short stories, some much shorter than others. You can skip the paragraphs of explanation or read them depending on your interest. My intention is to show that most fiction has germs of truth and authorial experience imbedded within. Few stories are built of whole, new cloth. Rather they are stitched from rags of memory, slices of experience, dreams both bad and good.

Chance encounters and observations of people and situations no matter how fleeting can be fuel for fiction. If your own writing has stalled out, don't despair. Try working from some point of reality or a long ago memory and see if a story lurks in the shadows.

This first story, The Bridge, was written after the old bridge across the Big Muddy River in Jackson County, Illinois was demolished. I lived on a farm next to the bridge and watched the day by day demolition of the structure. I had also watched the last years of deterioration afflicting the bridge. The school bus would stop before crossing and unload the students who would wait for the driver to cross the rumbling structure. The bus safely across, the driver would walk back to escort the kids across. Right down the center to avoid seesawing the loose deck boards

Mike and his family lived across the road. I remember the workers with their cutting torches straddling the iron beams and the day the bridge collapsed into the river before the last worker had time to dismount the structure. Mike, who was not old enough to ride the yellow school bus, often stood watching. The workers had no patience and cursed and swore at him when he got too close. The rest is fiction.

Perhaps you will find a germ of help in this book of stories.

Southern Illinois Alias Little Egypt

The Bridge

"That bridge is comin down today, lady," said the workman. He stood, legs apart as if he straddled some invisible barrier, the spokesman for the crew laboring above the river. "I promise."

Today. Could he really mean that? Leah wondered. The tone of his voice implied that the dirt and noise of the demolition team would continue indefinitely. She thought she would go mad trying to keep the house clean with the constant billows of dust they churned up. Leah retreated from the lip of the river, stepping carefully to avoid the muddy ruts. Change. How she hated it. Not only did they tear up the earth with their vile equipment, their whole intent was to destroy the old iron bridge.

Over the sound of heavy tools ringing against metal, Leah heard a roar and a backfire, then jumped back as a pickup truck rattled to a stop beside her. Billy Lee from down the road wrenched on the emergency brake and flicked a half-smoked cigarette out the window. Conscious of his inability to ever understand women, conscious of her desire to speak to him about the bridge, yet feeling too sick to think about it, he wondered why everyone picked on him when things went wrong.

"Mornin, Miss Leah. Mornin, Jack," said Billy Lee. He ratcheted open the driver's side door and climbed out. He looks hung over, Leah thought. His unshaven chin and sweat-streaked shirt made him look like a bum. The glare of the rising sun hurt his eyes. What was this woman complaining about now? Aloud, he said he'd see his sister, Robin, for a minute, have a cup of coffee, then join the work crew. Bitch, he thought, when he studied the prim, tight-lipped woman facing him across the morning. Meddling bitch. All his disgust, all his scorn for her was there in his blood-shot eyes; she recognized it, accepted it.

"How is Robin these days?" said Leah. She was glad of the diversion, but her thoughts quickly returned to the old, high topped bridge that was coming down today. It would be replaced by a sleek, concrete span a quarter of a mile downstream. She watched Billy Lee shuffle up to the fish shack where Robin lived with her five year old son, Mike.

Inside, Mike scrambled to finish his breakfast of cold pizza. He could hear his uncle outside. His stomach lurched with the sudden anxiety his uncle always inspired. His mother was still asleep after working her usual graveyard shift at the all night gas station. From the grass bare, junk-strewn yard Billy Lee hollered through the door, "Mike. Get your damn butt out here. Come help me lug this stuff to the bridge."

Stupid kid, he thought. Always in the way, always wantin to see what was goin on. The best way to deal with Mike was to keep him working, keep him under control. "Comin," answered Mike, "Ina minute." The expectant promise of the morning was suddenly tarnished. The electric feel of excitement in the air dampened with the need to jam the rest of his breakfast down as quickly as possible and get outside.

"Here, grab the hoses and clamps, boy," hissed Billy, "And don't drop nothin."

"Whacha doin? Is the bridge goin down today? You gonna cut the top off today? Can I help?" said Mike, all in a rush, fearing he wouldn't get another chance to ask. He looked around for the hoses Billy wanted. He knew he had to be quick or Billy would smack him one over the ear.

Over the growing din of the work site, Billy screamed, "Shut up, dummy, and get those things over here." Cringing, Mike scrambled across the yard with an armload of greasy hoses and dropped them on the pallet indicated by his uncle. Maybe he could do it good enough to please him this time. Mike imagined his uncle saying, good job, boy. Don't know what I'd do without such a good helper. He could picture himself firing up a cutting torch and playing the blue flame across the thick girder until it groaned free and dropped into the muddy water of the river. Without a father in his life, Billy filled that role much of the time. "Now, get out of here, boy. This's no place for a kid."

"I c ccan untangle these for you," said Mike. His fingers were already busy unweaving the maze of hoses and wires. He wanted desperately to stay, to watch the work, to feel the tools, to over-hear the cursing, the stories, to strut with the men, to be a part of the most exciting thing that had ever happened in his short life. Uncle Billy's rough voice interrupted his day dream.

"Get goin. Now. And don't let me see your face till supper time." Would that boy ever grow up to be worth a damn? Billy didn't think he had ever been that young and stupid. Intent on cupping his palm around the wind flicked match he held to his cigarette, he didn't notice Mike shrivel and back away into the brush along the river.

The boy retreated as far as an old deer bed. Here in the trampled grass he hunkered down to watch the workmen. The dismantling of the bridge progressed uneventfully until the approach of lunch time. Envious, Mike watched the men wielding their cutting torches to free the iron superstructure from the bridge pilings. He saw that three of the corners were free; one more cut would free the bridge from its pilings. A solitary worker sat high above the river, black, featureless against the glare of the sun. Amid the beams of the bridge top, he gripped an I-beam with his knees as if he rode some futuristic nag sunfishing the sky. Mike held his breath in anticipation. He was that workman against the sky. He was cutting through the last connector; his torch flared hot against the blue of the sky. The I-beam bucked like a demon steed and the sky turned over.

Mike didn't see Leah return to the river bank, but she noticed him hunched down in the flattened grass. Alarmed, she watched the boy for a few minutes before she moved for a better view of the bridge. By turning her head a little she could see both the child and the worker cutting through the beam. These people, she muttered to herself. Look how they destroy the past. She thought about the child in the grass, the child alone under the high dome of the sky. They destroy the past, then they blight their future.

In the deer bed Mike curled himself in a tight knot. *London Bridge is falling down, falling down*, he recited unheard in his hiding place. *London Bridge is falling down*, he sang with in a high tremulous voice, quickened with panicked fear. Through the mask of his fingers, he watched the huge bridge buck, then stand itself on end. He chanted another mantra of childhood, *Humpty Dumpty sat on a wall, Humpty Dumpty had a great fall. All the king's horses and all the king's men couldn't put*

Humpty together again. The bridge began its plunge into the muddy water. Falling, falling into the bowl of the sky that cupped him hard to the dry grass.

The bridge hit the water with a huge splash. *Old Johnny is dead and laid in his grave, laid in his grave, laid in his grave. Old Johnny is dead and laid in his grave...There grew an old apple tree over his head, over his head, over his head...the apples got ripe and ready to drop, ready to drop, ready to drop. The apples got ripe and ready to drop. Old Johnny is dead and laid in his grave, a long time ago.* Mike's voice rose to meet the screech of twisting metal. Old Johnny is dead? Leah wondered what was wrong with this child. His voice seems like a beacon of panic, a cry for help. She hardly heard the roar of the falling bridge as she wrapped her arms around the boy. For an instant Mike had been one with the workman riding the bucking iron through the sky into the water. He shut his eyes tight against the impact. Mikey is dead and laid in his grave, he murmurs. Leah holds him close and croons words of comfort.

Edward

Edward drifted into my life in late November. I first noticed him strutting through the trees on the hill behind the house. He preened and shuffled through the fall leaves, while I planted tulip bulbs in the raised bed by the garage. When Edward got bolder, he would stomp up and down the front deck, waiting for me to come outside. By Christmas he became so insistent I would find his blue face pressed against the glass door, watching me.

When I did go outside, he followed me everywhere, a brown streaky shadow. The neighbors began to notice and the mailman commented about my strange beastie, daily. The cats were outraged and refused to be consoled about this interloper.

When the weather turned nasty, I started leaving piles of cracked corn for Edward to munch. He deserted his nest in the woods and took to sleeping on the second floor deck railing, high above marauding dogs and coyotes. From this perch he could watch the TV through the sliding glass doors. He became incensed if I pulled the curtains before he was ready to tuck his head under his wing and sleep. He preferred action shows like *Magnum, P.I.* and *The "A" Team*. He nearly fainted at a rerun of *Snoopy's Thanksgiving*. Once I got used to his beady eyes peering over my shoulder, I enjoyed his company through the long winter evenings.

In the spring, while Edward roamed farther afield, amusing himself without me, he always came home in time to watch the *Evening News*. Until the 25th of July that is. Edward didn't come home that night. I searched for him the next day and the next. Looking for a twig colored creature in forty acres of brush was silly, but I did it anyway. *The Dukes of Hazard* wasn't very exciting without Edward.

On Saturday morning, I sat eating my breakfast of Grape-nuts with skim milk and three cups of black coffee. I read my dog-chewed *Southern Illinoisan*, certain that Edward had met the same fate as my newspaper.

A monstrous lot of squawking and gobbling interrupted my morbid imaginings. Running to the window, I saw Edward parading across the lawn, his neck arched and his tail spread like a Japanese fan. He ushered his black and white speckled lady, directing her timid progress with his out spread wings. In the circle of their mutual protection, peeping and scuffling, danced four downy, yellow children. Edward had brought his family home.

~~~~

In *"The Bridge"* and *"Edward,"* the location was dictated by my own location, a farm in the hill country of Southern Illinois. We had built a deck with a railing outside the sliding glass door. Just inside I had my work space complete with an easy chair and, something very new for us, a TV. Neighbors up the hill from us had an assortment of livestock which must have included turkeys. Our own animals were secured in various pens, cages, stables, and pastures, but others were not as thoughty and often allowed their livestock to roam the township.

This, I presume, was the plight of Edward. Heard rumors of Thanksgiving. Left home and needed a place to roost away from marauding dogs and coyotes.

~~~~

The Wrong Dog
Or When Is A Panther Not A Panther
{Or as Auntie Sally would say: "At big cat be a painter."}

The beagle-mix was a dump, a stray. Lacie noticed the mostly white dog nosing the trash on Monday. By Friday it had taken up with her neighbor's black hound. Lacie hated the black hound. She had caught him in the very act of killing one of her cats. The demon hound had crunched his huge teeth down on the cat's neck, then flipped the cat up and down until it died. Screaming and pelting the hound with rocks could not break his hold and in the end she had been unable to even recover the body because the black hound ran off with it to a secluded den amongst the kudzu covered rocks of a nearby pasture.

Now the bow-legged, splay-footed, white beagle was running with the demon hound. Too bad, thought Lacie. She had resolved to shoot the black hound the next time he crossed her property line. The rifle leaned ready by the kitchen door and Lacie did her chores in short intervals punctuated with long searching looks out across the field to check on the dogs. At noon the pair came trotting towards her barn. A quick look told Lacie her neighbor was gone, probably in town shooting pool with a slimy stogie clamped between his teeth. Lacie knelt and drew bead on the black dog, but as she squeezed off her shot the beagle leaped to meet the slug and the demon dog escaped with the ricochet in his hip. Dog screams cut the air as the two hurled themselves back across the road. Gut-shot, the beagle crawled under a corncrib. The hound limped in circles to bed down in the tall grass next to it. Lacie watched in disgust, then returned to her chores.

Next morning she knew the beagle still lived because the black hound kept vigil by the corncrib. Her neighbor had come home late and drunk and didn't notice the hound's bloody leg or the absence of the beagle. On the third day Lacie knew the beagle had died because the hound had given up his watch. She felt bad about its miserable death, but knew there was no remedy except silence. When she saw her neighbor, he said he thought a panther had done tore up his hound. Them painters gittin mighty froward he offered. Lacie opined she heard one scream in the night 'bout three day ago.

~~~~~

The Wrong Dog story is set on that same farm. The marauding dog lived across the road and the beagle migrated from one household to another staying a few weeks or a month before moving on. He must have had a set route because he would reappear about three months later. He ate with my cats, but refused to let anyone approach him. The black hound did kill my cat and carry it off to the rocky bluff in a nearby pasture, but I did not kill the beagle. I did make many attempts on the black dogs life, but he seemed to have had more than the allotted nine.

The legend that panthers roam Southern Illinois persists among the back country folk. They call them 'painters.'

~~~~~

~~~~~

The story that follows, the one about the two sisters, is set in the same framework. The language is part of the folk aura of the region. Memories of cleaning out an old house left by distant relatives is the basis for the scenes where the sisters are cleaning out their old home place. Making jam and jellies from wild May Apple, persimmon, paw paws, and other wild fruit was a natural part of the 'living off the land' culture that flourished in our part of Little Egypt.

~~~~~

Coral, Crystal, And The Broken Cat

"Papa musta kept everything he ever laid hands on." Coral used her shirt tail to wipe the sweat from her face. "I've never seen such a mess."

Coral's younger sister, Crystal, looked up from sorting old clothes, "Mama always said he was the saving kind."

"You remember him?" Coral added an armload of flattened cereal boxes to the trash heap in the middle of the attic floor. "Seems you were three when Mama took us back to Kentucky."

Unless you were bred, born, and wed in the scag-end of Illinois known as Little Egypt you were said to be from 'off.' Since the sisters had returned to Sandridge after a twenty year absence, the locals thought them newcomers and definitely from off.

"Course I remember," said Crystal.

A loud crash interrupted. A gray cat had slipped into the attic through a broken gable vent and landed on Coral's carefully sorted piles. Books, pictures, old receipts, and junk flew everywhere. She gasped and blinked, then grabbed the gray tom by the scruff of the neck and hurled him out the window.

"Damn cat. I've enough mess to clean up."

"Cats don't know better." Crystal scrambled to gather the toppled mess the cat had scattered across the attic floor. "I think he belongs to Mrs. Jerome up the hill."

"I catch him, he don't belong to nobody." Coral headed for the stairs. "A trap. I need a trap."

"Come back, Coral," yelled Crystal. "Don't be foolish."

The angry woman ran out the front door into the bare dirt yard. The gray cat ran under her feet, sending her sprawling in the dust.

"It's not a trap I need. It's a rifle." Coral slammed back into the house to find her papa's old 22 and a handful of shells.

"You can't shoot him. He's somebody's pet."

Coral didn't answer.

"Sister. What's Mrs. Jerome going to say?"

"She'll never know," said Coral.

"Course she'll know," said Crystal. "She knows everything."

"You're not to tell her, Crystal. Do you understand that?"

"She'll know. You're in trouble, sure."

"Tell and you'll be in trouble." Coral faced Crystal, then stepped closer. "Even a fish would stay out of trouble, if it kept its mouth shut."

A pearl blue Cadillac swept around the curve at the foot of Watt Hill and roared up the narrow road. Throwing gravel, the car stopped and backed down the hill to where Crystal stood by the mailbox, her run-down loafers planted firmly in the dust. She gaped at the elegant woman driving the car.

"Girl, have you seen a Persian cat?" Mrs. Jerome passed a printed handbill out the window. "I'm offering a reward. This will explain it. You can read, can't you?"

Crystal pursed her lips and stiffened her tongue, but no words appeared. She snatched the offered handbill and stepped back. The big car sped off.

"Grand Champion Lazarus Pom Pom de Jour of Whiskey Creek. Are you sure this is a cat, Crystal?" Coral peered at the handbill her sister had brought. "Who knew a cat could be a champion."

"She was so beautiful," said Crystal. "Like a queen."

"No." Coral slammed a plate down on the table. "The cat on this flyer is plumb ugly."

"Not the cat. Mrs. Jerome," said Crystal. "You killed her show cat. You killed it, Coral."

"Pug-nosed hair ball." Coral sipped her coffee. "Trespassing he was, leaving fleas and hair everywhere."

"Tell that to Mrs. Jerome." Crystal picked up her coffee, slopping a little on her dress. "There's a reward."

"Trouble will be our reward." Coral blotted the stain on her sister's dress with a tea towel. "It wouldn't do telling about a dead cat."

"It would set her mind at ease, knowing." Crystal read the handbill again, her finger underlining the words. "Reward for information, she says."

"How much reward?" Coral sat at the oak table after dropping the damp towel in the sink. "Money would find a home here, sure."

"Three hundred dollars."

Crystal stacked hot batty cakes on the chipped Blue Willow plates and brought them to the table with rashers of bacon and the syrup pitcher. "Buy a lot of pretties with three hundred dollars."

They sat in silence for awhile. Coral picked at a slice of bacon and a dry batty cake. "What did you put in these cakes? They're off some."

"Corn meal, egg, and drippin's like usual," said Crystal. She dug into a mound of hot cakes covered with bacon and syrup. Washing a mouthful down with a glass of milk thick with clotted cream, she said, "Your conscience is speaking through your appetite, Sister."

"You'll go see Mrs. Jerome?" Crystal scoured the cast iron skillet in the sink.

"We can't risk it." Coral sat back and crossed her long legs. "She holds a lien on this place."

"No. Can she take Papa's land?" Crystal dropped the heavy pan with a crash. "Maybe we made a mistake coming back here."

"Our land now." Coral chewed on a tendril of her

red-bronze hair. "I was hoping for an extension. Payment time is coming soon."

"The May Apples are ripe." Crystal appeared in the doorway of the shed where Coral sat sorting the few good tools from an abundance of trash. "Come quick, Sister, and bring a bucket."

"Picking wild fruit brews work." Coral frowned, deepening the creases around her mouth. "May Apples got to be scrubbed and chopped and sugared and stewed into jelly right off or they spoil. You know that."

"Varmints will get them tonight if we don't pick them now." Crystal made no move to leave. "That May Apple jelly is the very best. My mouth is practically dripping for a taste."

"Sorry," Coral began, but a car horn cut her thoughts. Straddling the deep ruts of the driveway, the blue Cadillac inched towards the house, its driver rapping the horn ring with her gloved hand.

"Your fence neighbor, Jackson Tyler, saw my cat on your porch yesterday." Mrs. Jerome leaned out the window of the car and pointed. "Where is Pom Pom?"

"Did Jackson get the reward?" asked Crystal.

"Hush." Coral pushed her sister aside and faced the powdered lady in the bright car. "We be fixin' to stir up a lickin' of May Apple Jelly. Sister, here, makes it the very best."

"We'll bring a glass by for you when it's set," said

Crystal, happy with Coral's change of heart. "It's the prettiest golden color."

"Jelly? I'm asking you about my cat." Mrs. Jerome's nostrils flared and faint red blotched her neck. "A gray, long-haired tom."

"All cats are gray in the dark," said Coral. "I expect he's dug in around here someplace."

"Well, be sure to call if you see him." Mrs. Jerome relaxed against the leather upholstery. "Better yet, let me leave some cans of Kitty Caress. You can put some out in clean dish and maybe he'll come to it."

"Sure thing." Coral accepted the cat food. "And maybe toads fly."

Next day the blue car returned. "Did Pom Pom come up to eat?" Mrs. Jerome patted her newly permed hair. "Do you have him?"

"Sister, run get a jar of jelly." Coral called. "One of those pert glasses from the filling station."

"Judson Tyler says he heard shooting over here."

"Jackson," corrected Coral. "Jackson Henry Tyler the fourth. What would he know."

Crystal brought the jelly. It was wrapped in a scrap of brown paper and tied with a twist of string.

"Thank you, I'm sure," said Mrs. Jerome. She held the parcel like it was a dead carp. "Do you own a gun?"

"Papa's old rifle." Coral shrugged. "Skunks and possum a plenty here."

"If someone has harmed my property, I'll have the

law on them." Mrs. Jerome flicked a dirt speck from her sleeve with manicured nails. "No one crosses me."

"Can she do that?" whispered Crystal. They watched the blue car back out of the drive. "Put us in jail?"

"Rich folk do as they please, Sister." As they watched the car glide up the hill road, a brown package flew out the window and landed in the water-filled ditch.

"She prowls around here all the time, now," said Crystal. "Gives me the fidgets."

"Stop pacing and help me move this box." Coral pushed the sweaty hair off her forehead. "She can't hurt you. It's me she'll be fumed at."

"We could find another cat. A twin to Pom Pom."

"Can't be two like that mug." Coral gave the box a final heave to settle it on the high shelf. "How about we dig the bugger up and leave it on Jackson Tyler's stoop?"

"Bad luck disturbing the dead." Crystal rapped the table with her knuckles. "We'd know real trouble then, haunted by a cat."

"Hush. Your mama would turn in her grave if she heard such nonsense."

"Cat food was gone this morning."

"A ghost cat eating Fancy Fish on our porch at Midnight. I don't think so."

"Jackson Tyler don't deserve our trouble." Crystal squinted at the house across the road. "He's a nice feller."

"I have to pay off that lien," said Coral. "This cat nonsense will steal our place away."

"Money," said Crystal. "Where'll we get the money?"

"I'll find it."

The next morning Coral, dressed for town, waited for Crystal to come in from doing the barn chores.

"Go wash up and change, Sister. The blue print dress and the black patent shoes. I'll comb up your hair when you're ready."

"You think it's okay to go off?" Crystal struggled with a button on her dress. "She might come and find the cat. Dig him up."

"Hold still. You got knots." Coral deftly smoothed Crystal's straight brown hair and twisted it into a bun. "There now. Get your purse."

Coral tucked a package under her arm, sorted through a batch of keys on a gritty string, and headed for the rusty truck parked behind the house.

"Where we going?" asked Crystal. She had to shout to be heard over the throaty roar of the truck's rusted out muffler. "We ought to get this thing fixed."

"You're going to the dime store lunch counter and get you something nice," said Coral. "I'm takin' care of business."

"If you don't get a ticket first." Crystal fanned herself with a hog-raising pamphlet she found on the peeling dash board. "Banana split or a chocolate soda.

How can I choose."

"Have both," said Coral. "You've got the egg money."

She pulled into the reserved space in front of the movie theater to let Crystal out.

"I'll meet you when I'm finished. Have fun."

She eased the coughing truck into the traffic flow and headed east on Walnut Street towards the city parking lot. She had a stop to make before heading across the street to First Trust and Loan.

The neon sign reading Jack's Coin and Pawn flashed in the noon sun.

"Can I help you?"

"I was wondering what silver certificates bring now?" Coral fiddled with the rubber band around the cigar box she clutched to her chest. "You know, those old dollar bills with the blue seals?"

"Depends on condition and series number."

"Condition?" Coral seemed surprised. She placed the box on the glass counter and opened it. She stared at the thick wad of old bills as if she had never seen them before. "They should look good?"

"Yes, crisp, mint-condition blue seal bills can be valuable to collectors."

"How about old coins, like from the war?" Coral removed a flat metal container from the cigar box and shut the lid on the greasy, faded dollar bills. "From the

Philippines and Germany, even."

"No value there I'm afraid. Mostly stuff that kids collect. I'd give you $10 for that Luck Strike Green flat pack, though."

"Maybe next time." Coral slipped the box into her pocket. "Sorry to bother you."

"Can you cash these savings bonds?" Coral sat down at an expanse of polished desk across from a sharp faced man. "And these certificates of deposit?"

"Twenty-five dollar Pearl Harbor issue bonds. Goodness, these haven't drawn interest in years."

"You mean they aren't worth anything?" Deep lines etched Coral's face. "How can that be?"

"No, no, I can cash them for you. They certainly are beautiful. No steel engravings on modern bonds."

"How about the CD's?" Coral hardly noticed the detailed commemorative pictures on the crisp bonds laying on the desk. "Papa bought them just before he died."

"You know there is a penalty if you cash the CD's before the maturity date?"

"Yes." Coral fiddled nervously with the buttons on her jacket. "I need the money, now."

"Let me figure the penalty." He scratched out some figures and checked a table of fine print numbers. "It comes to $182.68. Are you sure?"

"Cash them," said Coral. "Now."

"If that's what you want." Coral barely noticed that

the banker paid the value of the bonds from his own pocket and carefully stashed them in his briefcase.

Crystal was waiting outside when Coral returned. "Sorry I'm late."

"Did you get the money?"

"Got some, lost some," said Coral. She held out the penalty slip and a traffic ticket for defective equipment.

"Almost two hundred dollars to get our own money, and forty-five dollars for the ticket." Crystal sucked in her lower lip. "New muffler don't cost much more than the ticket."

"I did what I had to." Coral Lee wheeled the truck back into the street without signaling. "Try to understand."

"More than you know, Sister. Where we going?"

"You have a nice time?" Coral asked.

"Saw Jackson Tyler." Crystal smiled a bit. "He sat with me."

"You talked to him?" Coral nearly ran a stop light. "You didn't tell about the cat?"

"He bought me ice cream." Crystal hugged herself. "He's a sweet feller."

"I don't know what's got into you."

"Jackson has a broody hen." She watched the unrolling fields and hills. "He's going to let me borrow her. Hatch me a clutch of chicks."

Coral eased the truck up the curving drive and stopped in front of the sprawling white house.

"You think this is Mrs. Jerome's house?" Her lower lip quivered noticeably. "Blue Cadillac's not here."

"Rich people don't leave their cars outside." Coral pointed to the four-car garage attached to the lower side of the tall house. "Probably in there."

"Garage is twice the size of our house." Crystal applied pink lipstick using the truck's crazed side mirror. "Are we really going in there?"

"Powder your nose, too." Coral Lee grabbed her pocketbook and headed up the front walk. "Hurry."

Coral pushed past the housekeeper. Slamming doors and peering into empty rooms, she made her way through the house with Crystal tagging along behind. By the time they burst through the French doors onto the patio, Crystal was gasping for breath.

"Good afternoon, ladies." Mrs. Jerome rose from her wrought iron garden settee. "A surprise, I'm sure."

Facing the regal woman across a table set with a silver tea service and Royal Dalton china, Coral could only mumble, "Money. We came about the money."

"Money? Are you still trying to collect the reward?" Mrs. Jerome rang a bell on the tea tray. "Hildie will see you out."

"No. Wait." Coral struggled to gain control. "We came to...."

"The cat got in the attic," Crystal wheezed. "He tripped Coral."

"Please leave, now." Mrs. Jerome's diamonds flashed as she pointed towards the road.

"At the bank they said there'd be no problem." Coral put her pocketbook down amidst the tea cakes and began searching for her wallet. "Got it here somewhere."

"Sister didn't mean to." Without thought, Crystal picked up a monogrammed linen napkin and wiped the sweat from her forehead and upper lip. "It sure is hot. You got one of them air conditioner things to cool off your house?"

"Hildie, call the sheriff." Mrs. Jerome rang the bell again. "Ladies, this conversation is over."

"Here's the money." Coral pulled a wad of bills from her jacket pocket and waved it about. "Take it."

"We shouldn't of buried him." Crystal flung the napkin aside. "Are you going to put us in jail?"

Mrs. Jerome reached across the table and grasped Coral"s wrist. "Calm down, please."

"Don't hurt her." Crystal lunged towards Mrs. Jerome and knocked over the tea pot. "Hateful, old cat deserved what he got."

"Shut your mouth, Crystal." Trying to free her wrist, Coral bumped the table and sent tea cups crashing to pieces on the stone patio. "Hope those weren't your Sunday best."

"Out, now," shrieked Mrs. Jerome. "You'll have a bill for the damages tomorrow."

"Mercy. Comes the devil his self." Crystal turned sheet white and swooned across the tea table.

Looking past her stricken sister to the edge of the garden, Coral saw the ghost that felled Crystal. A smug gray cat stood watching her.

"Lazarus Pom Pom." Mrs. Jerome relaxed and smiled at the approaching cat. "Come to Mama, Pom Pom."

"How come he's here?" Stunned, Coral nearly dropped her teeth at the sight of the trouble-making animal. "This cat supposed to be lost."

"No. Pom Pom came home last night." She picked up the purring cat and held him over her shoulder like a baby. "Such a pretty puss."

"This is to pay off the lien." Coral laid the roll of money on the settee. "The money you loaned Father."

"Oh, that. A pittance." Mrs. Jerome slipped the bills into her pocket and walked to the French doors. "Now leave. You've had your say."

"Come on, Crystal." Coral helped her sister up and brushed off the crumbs. "Let's go home."

"Guess these fishes didn't keep their mouths shut enough." Crystal tried to tidy her hair. "Can we stop and get Jackson's broody hen on the way home."

"We better head home and clean up before we go calling." Coral started the truck with a jerk. "Can't let your beau see you looking like a mad hussy."

"Evening, Mr. Tyler." Coral held the edge of the screen door with one hand and a covered dish with the other. "Sister made an extra bait of cherry cobbler. Thought you might like some."

"I brought a box for the hen," stammered Crystal. "If you're still willing I take her."

"Come in, ladies." Jackson Tyler made room on the kitchen table for the cobbler. "Smells real good."

"Looks like rain." Coral put the dish on the table and removed the napkin. "We could use it."

"Got some ice cream," said Jackson. "Care to set a bit and have a dish with me?" Taking their silence assent, Jackson got bowls from the cupboard and went to the freezer on the back porch for the ice cream.

"What's wrong?" Jackson was surprised by the look of horror he saw on his guests' faces when he returned with the ice cream. "Are you all right?"

"That cat. That's Mrs. Jerome's cat." Coral pointed to the long-haired cat following at Jackson's feet. "Why is he here?"

"Yeah, why?" echoed Crystal. "He's dead and gone."

"Ladies, meet Smokey." Jackson smiled. "Guess he does take after his pappy. That old rogue has kin all over these hills."

Elle and Stinkin Joe

The heavy sky watches a bleak cabin hunched beside the interstate. Fronds of primitive fern grow rank up to the pollution zone fringing the shoulder of the highway where crunchy, oil-oozing blacktop announces the six lanes of concrete snaking across the ruptured landscape to the city. The heavy sky, holding back urgent rain, watches the tortured man reach out to the brittle-pretty woman on the porch of the cabin. She twists away and hunches over the porch railing. Preparing to release its moisture on the waiting land, the sky feels the pain radiating from the man and woman on the cabin porch. It holds back its rain for a space of time.

"Snap out of it, Elle." The man walks across the weathered boards to the trembling woman. He grasps her by the shoulders and shakes her gently. The he wraps her in his arms and tries to walk her through the open door of the silent cabin. His lips form the syllables, please, please God. Aloud he says, "Let's go inside, love. The rain's a coming."

Elle turns in his arms to stare at him, blank-faced and soul bare. A thin whimper crosses her hard-pursed lips. "I can't go in there, Joe." Stinkin Joe, a smile almost makes it to her lips and she closes her eyes to remember her mother-in-law explaining how Lincoln Joseph Davis became Stinkin Joe before the end of his first day at school. Then other bright pictures crowd her mind to bar the way into the cabin. She watches them scroll across the back of her closed eyelids. Amanda, beautiful Amanda with her dark-tangled hair and summer honey skin, plays on the kitchen floor, beating her soup-pot drum and flashing her sunshine smile at everyone. Amanda, lovely Amanda with oatmeal in her eyebrows, learning to feed herself. Sweet, tender Amanda twisting stems of wildflowers into streamers for the ones she loves. Elle repeats her plea, "I can't, Stinkin Joe. I can't go in there."

"This ain't doing us no good, Elle." Stinkin Joe presses her head against his crisp shirtfront. He wonders if he will ever have his lively, lovely Elle again. Maybe he left her beside that cold mound of earth in Mt. Moriah. Maybe they put her spirit in that dark hole with the small white box. Feeling hot tears soak through his shirt, he remembers the fragile woman in his arms and says, "Elle, woman, you got to come back. Come back to your ever-loving man."

"Go away, Joe." Elle leans back against his arm and tries to focus her tear-wracked eyes on his face. Who is this man with Amanda's tangle of kinky-dark hair and honey smooth skin? She studies his eyes. The whites, vivid-bright against his skin, are bloodshot, his pupils dilated pools of brown shadow. Running from her pain for a little space of time, Elle throws herself into the pool of his eyes and remembers. Remembers the three of them rolling in a field of golden poppies, laughing until their sides hurt. Hugging Joe and laughing at Amanda's discovery of woolly worms and sunlit petals of silky smooth flowers. Remembers screaming in delight and clinging together all three on the rollercoaster at the county fair. The nutmeg scent of Stinkin Joe's aftershave reaches down through the pool of Elle's remembering. She knows he only wears aftershave when he goes to church, but it's workday Tuesday and the order of her universe has been toppled and torn and stretched beyond her belief. "Hold me, please hold me." Her fingers dig into his back, trying to burrow through the rough tweed of his jacket to find heart and soul. She mashes her smooth cheek hard against the lapels guarding his chest. "Harder, Joe, harder, please."

He crushes Elle's thin body to his chest, trying to absorb her grief, to suck it up like a sponge. "I'm sorry, Elle." Over her blond head he can see the long weedy lawn roll down to the freeway where a steady roar of traffic pours across the landscape. Carefully, tenderly he rubs her shoulders and the special place where her shapely skull rises from the column of her neck. Kneading and probing her stiff, unyielding muscles, he winces as his eyes travel to the broken place in the chain link fence that marks the boundary between the road and the lawn. He tries not to remember the day the road construction gang put up the heavy fence that marked the opening of the new interstate. Shuddering at the memory, he turns away and guides Elle into the cabin. "Come along, Elle. You need some rest."

The rain fraught sky watches them walk into the dim room holding to each other. Its black clouds let go of a few rain drops. They splatter on the cabin's corrugated tin roof and glisten the thick blades of grass around the cabin. The afternoon breeze freshens into wind that bends the row of hollyhocks low across the garden fence. No one hears the wind clash the swing chain against the frame of the play set in the side yard. No one except the sky with its waiting storm.

Inside, Stinkin Joe propels Elle across the room to the bed in the corner. A wedding ring quilt, worked in tones of green, gold, and rose on pristine white, covers the bed. He thinks of the long evenings his mother worked on that quilt, while he studied for the civil service exams. She knew he would ask Elle to marry him once he had passed the exams and she wanted the quilt ready as her wedding gift for them. He's glad his mother isn't here to see the smaller quilt with its hobby horse pattern obscured by muddy stains crumpled on the floor near the cot across the room. Hard as he tries not to notice, it draws his eyes like a magnet. An invisible hand squeezes his heart and threatens to stop its very beating.

He wonders, if it hurts him this much, how can Elle stand it. And how can she bear the emptiness of the room. He carefully slips her black wool jacket from her slumped shoulders, then works it down past her elbows. He finds no comfort in the rough scratchy material, but buries his face in it to drink her scent before he folds the jacket across the back of chair. Her woodsy sweet perfume carries him back, back to their courting time, when he drove his mother's rusted Buick down the elm-lined street to pick up his girl. His girl, his Elle, sitting close under his arm as he drove the huge old car to the dance. He remembers feeling giddy with the promise of it all. Elle's muffled sob pulls him back from the spot lit dance floor to the dim cabin. "Elle, let me get you something to eat."

"I'm not hungry." Elle sits down on the bed with motions slow and weary as an old, old woman. She stares hard at her own hands so she won't have to see the child-size table and chairs in the kitchen corner of the one room cabin. How can this be happening? Surely her lightfoot daughter will come dancing through the front door with chains of daisies woven in her hair.

Where are you, God? God, we've been good. Maybe it's all a bad dream. A dream she'll wake up from soon. She lays down on the bed and turns her face to the wall.

"I'll heat some soup." He bends over to pat Elle's shoulder and stroke her baby-fine hair back from her forehead. Straightening up, he gazes at her for a moment before going to the cupboard to find a can of soup. He thinks about his wife; she looks so small, so still, so alone on the big bed, curled on her side against the wall with her long fingers clenched into fists. Fists to hold the good thoughts close, perhaps. Fists to drive away the demons. He moves quietly, cat-like to disturb her as little as possible while he rummages in the cupboards for the soup, a sauce pan, and the can opener. Amanda, he remembered, didn't care much for soup. He grins a little as he hears her in his mind's ear telling them soup was much too runny and she couldn't eat it with her fingers.

The everyday kitchen sounds lull Elle into a light doze somewhere on the edge of waking and sleeping. A child in yellow knee socks and sneakers with flashing lights in the heels slips into her mind. The dark-eyed child comes skipping into her unconscious, calling, Mommy, Mommy, can I go outside now? Please, Mommy. I'll be good. I'll play on the swing. In slow motion, her slender legs carry her out the door before Elle can answer. Elle knows she must follow, must follow, must stop the laughing child, must call her back, but her mouth refuses to form the words or let any sound come through her waiting lips. She tries to run after the little girl, but her legs refuse to move faster than a snail crawl across a room that seems to grow bigger and bigger. The harder she pushes herself to follow, the slower she moves. She tries to scream, but she feels like she is drowning in the thick air. She struggles with unseen hands that try to pin her to the bed. She must get up. She must catch up to Amanda. She must stop her, keep her safe, hold her close.

"Come and eat, Elle." Stinkin Joe shakes the dozing woman gently and rolls her over on her back. He lies down on the bed beside her and nuzzles her cheek and neck. He kisses her awake with the hope that she has had a little peace, a space of rest and relief from the bleakness of reality. He is startled at the violence of her waking. "Easy, easy now, Elle."

The woman on the bed flails at him with fists and elbows. Her mouth opens in a silent scream. He can barely hold her from falling off the bed as she thrashes wildly. Finally she manages to thrust herself upright, awake, and her silent scream becomes audible. "Come back, come back, Amanda, come back." Unable to get past the man beside her on the bed, she scrambles down over the footboard and stands shaking on the cold linoleum. "Where are my shoes? I got to go look for her."

"She's gone, Elle." Stinkin Joe stands up and tries to wrap his arms around her waist and lead her to the table. "Come have some soup. Maybe you'll feel better." Strong beyond the ordinary, Elle twists away from him. Fear for her wells up in his throat like the bitter bile of sickness.

"I've got to go after her." Elle shuffles her feet into her shoes and runs out of the room, drawn by the dancing yellow knee socks and the flashing sneakers of her dream. I can't see her face thinks Elle. Why can't I see her face? Panic chokes her, stops the very breath in her chest, sends her spinning through the door. I've got to see her face.

"Wait, Elle. It's raining." Stinkin Joe tries to get a grip on Elle's cold hand. He has to keep her safe, safe from the sudden disaster that drops from nowhere. She is his light, his center. Surely the terrible memories will fade and they will get on with their life together. Have another baby. Bad enough to go on without Amanda, but without Elle, that is unthinkable. He lunges out the door and manages to grab her wrist.

"Elle, I love you."

"I'm sorry, Joe." The desperate woman throws off his hand and stumbles down the porch steps. Her trembling legs threaten to drop her onto the wet lawn. The heavy sky can wait no longer. The whirl of low clouds explodes black rain and pelts Elle soaked before she can take ten steps. Her gray blouse clings transparent over her shoulders and breasts. Her nylons darken with the rain pounding against her frail body. At the bottom of the steps she stops and turns to look back, blindly at the cabin. Suddenly she knows, she knows she won't find Amanda on the swing or playing in the flowers, ever. Barely audible above the storm, she shouts back at

Stinkin Joe, "Why did it happen? Why, Joe, why?" She turns towards the freeway and begins to run through the wet grass. Faster and faster she races over the slight downhill of the lawn. She slows only to strip off her shoes which are threatening to trip up her running feet. Her feet, bare except for the shredding nylons, move silent over the muddy, rutted grass where the log truck had torn the earth and the fence, torn her heart away. Only the black rain hears her scream. Only the rain and Stinkin Joe.

From the porch steps he sees Elle hurl herself towards the highway. As he watches her disappear into the rain, Joe can only follow. He is almost too shocked to act, but his feet move without command from his stalled brain. Down the steps and into the rain he runs. He crosses the puddled grass and splashes through the muddy ruts to the broken place in the fence. He remembers yesterday's Elle, all light and laughter and dancing feet. The memory blinds him for an instant to the rush of traffic so close beyond the crushed fence. So close is the flow of cars and trucks he feels the sting of flung rain on his face. "Where are you, Elle? Elle, come back."

A glare of lightning shows him the highway clear as day. As clear as the afternoon the log truck tore out of control across the median and through the chain link. Through the fence and onto his green lawn the heavy loaded truck came. It gouged deep ruts in the soft earth, gouged deep ruts in his soul. The loaded truck tumbled its logs across the highway and across his lawn. Heavy, crushing logs. Mammoth logs smashing the swing set. The apocalyptic vision dims his view of rumbling log trucks and tankers beating down this long, straight stretch of the interstate. Blocks his view of a huge rig bearing down on his small, soaked misery of a woman running along the shoulder of the highway. Where is she going? What is she doing? A flash of lightening and the drum of thunder brings him back, back to Elle. He hears her scream on the storm wind, thin and piercing.

"Come back, Elle." Stinkin Joe cups his hands around his mouth to answer. "Come back."

Looking back, Elle sees her man in the daylight of another lightening flash. He stands raving on the spot lit shoulder of the interstate. He looks like some oversized praying mantis in his funeral black and skinny, long legs and arms. He seems to be dancing and calling. What could he have to do with her? Her long blond hair is plastered to her skull and her black crepe skirt is one with the rain and mud thrown up by the passing trucks. Elle stops and stands on the shoulder of the highway. "Amanda. Amanda." Empty eyed, she rides the edge. The trucks blow their air horns and screech their brakes, but Elle hears only the scream in her head, the scream of her child, Amanda. The scream in her head becomes the scream from her own warped mouth.

Stinkin Joe comes rushing through the black rain,

but there is nothing left except the scream.

~~~~~

The story of Elle and Stinkin Joe has its roots in a ten second view from a speeding car on a trip over a monotonous freeway. If you think driving hundreds of miles on a straight string freeway can't inspire a story, then think harder. A brief glimpse of a lone house overlooking a new section of roadway provided the inspiration for this story. Much of the front yard taken for the road left a rusting swing set teetering near the right away. It was not hard to conjure up a family whose search for peace and safety was thwarted by progress and big machines.

Joe's nickname came from a battered notebook I had kept as a child. I copied odd or interesting names from the local newspaper, school yard teasing sessions, billboards, and conversations. I always had an ear out for new names to add to my collection. The list was long partly because we lived near the Indian reservation, partly because of the influx of migrant workers every summer. The folks from the rodeo crowd and the traveling carnivals and circuses gave me more fuel for my list. Not a bad hobby. Cheap too.

~~~~~

The Two Happiest Days in a Man's Life

Howard 'Hop' Hopkins felt a stab of excitement run up his sternum. He was about to sign on the dotted line and become owner of the brand new Chartcraft 500 perched on its trailer in the Crow Cove Marina parking lot. For the last eleven years Hop had worked a desk job at the post office where the main topics of conversation were football and fishing. It always made him feel like a second class citizen because he hated football and was the only senior male employee who didn't own a boat. Now, that was about to change. Hop stretched like an old tom cat and popped his knuckles. He smoothed his T-shirt down over an ample beer belly and sat down across from the salesman.

Hop could just see himself telling his fellow workers about the monster fish he was going to catch from his new boat. He was getting into the part where the fish nearly bent his rod double, when the salesman placed the contract on the desk for Hop's John Hancock.

A spread of shock reddened Hop's face when he read the final figure on the bottom of the sales sheet.

"How'd the price get that high?" He drummed his fingers on the glass desk top. "I thought we had a deal."

The salesman adjusted his cuff links and carefully placed a pen next to Hop's right hand. "Yes, of course, Mr. Hopkins. But there's always sales tax." He cleared his throat. "And delivery charges. Preparation charges. A paperwork fee. I hear the bass are really biting over on Black Oak."

Hop stretched his pudgy fingers toward the pen. It was one of those promo-pens with company advertising on its barrel. This one read Inlet Boats, Sales and Service. "No bass for me. I'm going for the big guys, channel cat and flatheads." He picked up the ball point and nervously clicked the retractor in and out. "I sorta intended to pay cash, but I'm a little short of that figure."

The salesman reached a glossy calendar from a stack behind his desk and laid it open beside the contract. Full color trophy fish leaped and swam through the months to add to his pitch for the sleek boat outside. "No problem. We can write it up as a time contract. Just a few hundred down and you hook up and drive off with the Chartcraft 500." He flipped the calendar to July where a huge flathead hung by its tail for a record shot. "This the sort of fish you going for? Use the rest of the cash to spiff up your equipment. New rod? Gear bag? Lures? Fishfinder?"

Without another qualm Hop signed the amended contract with a flourish. No need to tell Willie Fay about the extra expense. Why, with all the fish he was going to catch, the boat would practically pay for itself.

An hour later Hop loaded the rest of his purchases into the Chartcraft which rode high and proud on its trailer. The deep red boat with white scrolling along its bow had been hooked to the back of his pickup while he shopped. The one hundred and fifty-nine smackers he had to lay out for the new hitch and hook up galled him for awhile. He knew he could have got it for half at Sears, but then he couldn't have brought the boat home until Monday. His gloomy mood evaporated when he hefted the new casting rod.

Though he knew his old casting rod was more than adequate, this new one was a beaut, and of course he needed life vests. Willie Fay would never go out in the boat with him unless she had the right safety equipment. An oversize cooler and a Jim Dandy bait bucket fit snugly behind the bow seat. Rain slickers, a box of treble hooks, landing net, and fish keeper followed. Amazing, the amount of stuff a fellow needed to catch a fish, but no matter. This was really living. Hop trembled with excitement when he thought about telling the guys at work about his new toy. Maybe he could get his neighbor, Jenkins, to snap an instant picture of it so he could show it around, proof of his bragging rights.

Much to Hop's surprise his truck with the boat in tow barely managed to negotiate the small hill on the road from the marina to the highway. It was better on the smooth blacktop where he concentrated on minimizing the fish-tailing of the trailer and remembering to corner more carefully. Things went pretty well until he turned down the hilly township road towards home. On the first rise the pickup lugged badly and emitted odd growly noises from the vicinity of the transmission. Hop was sweating by the time his driveway hove into view, but he forgot his worries at the sight of home and Willie Fay waiting in the yard.

Willie Fay arched her plucked eyebrows in surprise when she saw Hop pulling the shiny new boat into the driveway. Gosh, she must have forgotten it was the day he was bringing the boat home or had Hop jumped the gun by a week. She hoped he had remembered her stamps with all the excitement of buying the boat. She couldn't wait to be the first to show the new stamp to her friends. She tugged her tight skirt lower on her thighs, then picked her way across the gravel trying to avoid stepping on the sharper rocks with her thin soled gold slippers. She patted her beehive of jet black hair with one hand and waved a greeting to her husband with the other. "Did you bring it, Hop?"

The old girl had been a looker in her day, thought Hop, but that blue eye-crap was too much. Where had the years gone? He pulled on the hand brake and climbed out of the truck. "Come and have a look, Willie Fay." Funny how it was suddenly important to have his wife's approval of his new purchase.

She minced around to the trailer and stroked her white hand along the scrolling on the side of the boat. Her talon-like nails matched the red of the boat perfectly. "Right purty ain't she, Hop?" She strained to see over the side of the boat to watch Hop unloading his new fishing equipment. "Did you remember my stamps, Hop? My Elvis stamps. Please say you remembered."

Hop caressed the fishing rod and focused his eyes on the roll of fat threatening to escape the waist band of Willie Fay's black skirt. Damn, he knew there was something he was supposed to bring home. That blasted Elvis stamp was going to cost him. "I got busy."

Willie Fay's face seemed to collapse like a punctured balloon. Her lower lip quivered and a tear furrowed down her cheek through the mascara and pancake makeup. "Aw, Hop, can't I trust you to do anything?" Her indifference towards the new boat turned to anger and for an instant she hated Hop so deeply she could taste the bitter gall in the back of her throat. She swallowed it back and turned up the walk to the house. "Supper's ready when you are," she hollered over her shoulder.

Hop knew his wife's stiff-backed, "don't touch me" walk well enough. He didn't try to follow her. He finished unloading his new gear, then unhooked the trailer from his truck. He'd get up early tomorrow morning and take the boat out on the river. Unlike the trek to the lake, it would be less than a mile with no hills. He figured he could launch at the old road cut on Jenkin's place next door. Should be a piece of cake since the Big Muddy was high this time of year. He'd figure out the towing problem later. He supposed he could use Willie Fay's Buick. That old V-8 could haul a double wide. Unfortunately it drove like a bathtub and besides, it was pink with a row of fuzzy animals in the rear window.

The thought of putting the boat into the water for the first time pushed the pink car with its load of stuffed animals out of Hop's mind. He was whistling when he entered the kitchen. He hardly noticed his wife's scowl when he left a trail of equipment across the porch, the laundry room and into the kitchen. It never occurred to him that she would be upset with a fine new bait box on the supper table or life vests on the dryer or the new casting rod propped across the rocker. Hop washed up and took his place at the table.

Biting her tongue Willie Fay passed Hop the biscuits. Somebody had to keep the peace around this house and it looked like it was going to be her job, as usual. She asked, "You going fishin tomorrow?" She handed him the butter and got up to get the fried chicken and gravy.

Hop didn't answer until he had drowned his biscuits in the pepper-flecked milk gravy. He studied the globs of melted butter surfacing around the edges of his plate. "Of course. You coming?" It sure couldn't hurt to have another pair of hands along to help with the launching, he thought. Then he took a good look at

Willie Fay's finger nails and almost choked. Guess he hadn't really looked at the old girl for awhile. "How the hell do you get anything done with those claws, woman?"

Willie Fay was pleased that Hop noticed her nails. She had been cultivating them for months. She buffed them on her shoulder and answered, "Very carefully." Maybe she would go fishing with him. Out in the boat they could talk without Hop sticking his face in the newspaper or falling asleep in front of the TV. She could picture herself in a scene from a favorite soap opera, billowy scarf floating in the breeze, trailing her hand in the water as the boat drifted along.

After supper Hop and Willie Fay sat watching "Wheel of Fortune." While Willie Fay tried to second guess the puzzle answers, Hop rigged a bottom hook with a couple of treble hooks. After he finished the new rod he went to the garage for his old one and rigged it the same way. Good thing he had bought a new rod because Willie Fay would need his old one. Hop felt light, energized. He'd tell her about the time payments later, after she saw how much fun the new boat was going to be.

During a commercial Willie Fay watched Hop thread and tie the fine leader to the hooks. She stubbed her smoke out in the ceramic ash tray she had made in art class and lit up another. "What kinda fish, Hop?" She needed to know what he'd expect her to cook, didn't she?

Those didn't look like hooks for bluegill and that was the only kind of fish she'd ever cooked. A worm of ash dropped to her ample bosom unnoticed. She repeated her question when Hop failed to responded.

Hop leaned the finished rods against the wall next to the velvet painting of Elvis. Willie Fay had painted it in one of the classes she was always running off to. Damn junk, he thought. She's got to stop bringing home all this clutter so I can breathe. Aloud he said, "Now I got to rustle up some bait. Those channel cat like really stinky bait. Really, really stinky." He went to the kitchen to look in the fridge. He could see himself standing in his new boat reeling a gleaming, fighting whopper of a cat close enough for Willie Fay to net it. "Hot dogs, or liver, maybe." He found an open package of wieners in the back of the fridge.

Willie Fay yelled at Hop, "Why not worms or those little plastic things?" She tried to remember about cooking cat fish. Filleted and fried, stuffed and baked, stewed into a court bouillon? Ugh. She much preferred the captain's platter at the Anchor Fast Fish Shop. A new thought nagged its way into her mind. Her canasta partner, Stella, might be at the lake with her husband and their boat was old, faded and out of style.

Next morning Hop loaded the pickup and hitched up the new boat. He was irked, but not surprised at the stuff his wife thought essential for a morning of fishing.

Her cushions and sunblock were stowed under the seat. An umbrella, makeup kit, extra shoes, and nylon jacket used space Hop felt belonged to his fishfinder and landing net. Willie Fay's jug of ice tea shared cooler space with the bag of moldy hot dog and liver chunk bait Hop had concocted. There had been a minor argument about whether the stink from the bait would make the tea taste funny, but he had won that one. He was sorry he didn't have time to whip up a batch of bourbon soaked chicken liver dough balls he had read about in True Fisherman magazine.

Hop sat in the truck for ten minutes while Willie Fay checked the doors and the coffee maker and made sure the cat was out. He couldn't decide if he wished she would hurry up or change her mind and stay home. When she finally hoisted her spandex clad butt into the seat next to him, Hop grunted and turned the radio on with the volume high. That should cover any strange noises the truck might make, he thought. He eased the pickup out of the driveway and headed for the blacktop. Everything went along fine, until he put on his blinker to turn onto the Jenkin's place.

Willie Fay sat up straight and waved a monster fingernail under Hop's nose. "Where you going?" She bobbed around in the seat like some black-helmeted hit me toy. "Lake's that way."

"Um, I thought we'd take the boat out on the river. There's an easy place to launch at the Jenkin's place."

Hop was puzzled. What difference could it make to her where the boat was launched?

Willie Fay won that battle with a clinching argument about concession stands and restrooms at the lake. She didn't mention the hope that some of her canasta group would be at the lake to see the new boat. It would take some of the sting out of not having the Elvis stamp to show off. Hop didn't mention his fear about the pickup's transmission either, so they were even.

At the lake Hop waited his turn to back the truck down the boat ramp. By the time he had wrestled the boat trailer down the concrete ramp, sweat rivualed his body. Though he had studied the instructions for backing a trailer, he had never actually done it. He had ignored Willie Fay when she told him to practice in the driveway.

"How hard can it be?" Hop had asked her. "You just turn in the opposite direction you want to go."

"Don't say I never told you." Her words sounded in his head so loudly he thought she was telling him again. Hop was surprised when he realized Willie Fay had been silent all the while he was backing the trailer down the ramp. He wiped the sweat from his upper lip, turned off the ignition, and said, "Close enough."

Willie Fay opened her door and slid out. "Looks like you need another six feet. I'm going potty while you get lined out." She turned and headed towards the concession area.

By the time Willie Fay returned with a sack of Chock-O-Mallow candy bars Hop was cursing the air blue. The red boat was sitting at an awkward angle, half in the water, half on the trailer, with Hop trying to keep it from overturning onto the ramp. What's the big idiot gone and done now, wondered Willie Fay. You wouldn't think getting a boat in the water could be such a big deal.

Hop spied his wife waltzing down the ramp with her sack. She sure took her own sweet time getting here. "Where you been?" he hollered. "Jeez, McGeez, you're never around when I need you. Come and grab this side so I can guide it into the water." With Willie Fay to steady the boat Hop was able to slide it into the water right side up. He felt like he'd put in a week of hard labor by the time he finally climbed aboard his new boat and took a seat aft where he could operate either the Power Stud engine or the little trolling motor. A surge of pride ran up his spine when he rubbed his hands along the smooth contours of the sixty horse engine.

Willie Fay reclined in the bow, nested in a pile of cushions with the bag of candy bars at her left hand and her vodka-laced jar of ice tea on her right. She sipped ice tea and watched Hop start the big engine. Now that the hard work was done they could enjoy themselves. The red boat sped away from the shore with a tremendous roar. "Stop showing off, Hop." The sudden acceleration sloshed tea down her blouse front and splattered her glasses. Leave it to Hop to mess up a simple thing like starting the boat.

When he finally had the boat under control, Hop ventured a look at his wife. She was jamming a second candy bar into her mouth. Geez, he thought, she's a regular blimp in that life vest. Aloud he said, "Do you have to eat all the time?" He jockeyed the boat into one of the deep inlets of the lake and switched to the trolling motor. "Time to get our lines in the water." He handed one of the rods to Willie Fay and started threading hot dog chunks on his own.

Willie Fay clamped her red talons around the cork grip of her rod and said, "Please, Hop, fix mine, too." Her voice sounded small and shrill in the expanded atmosphere over the water. When she got no response from Hop, she gave the rod a limp tweak that sent the line drooping over the side of the boat.

"You got to bait the hook first," snorted Hop. "Reel it in and do it right."

Willie Fay looked up at her husband. Rather than answer him, she tucked the pole under one flabby knee and produced a pack of cigarettes from her purse. After she lit up, she removed her glasses. That's better, she thought. To her soft, unfocused gaze Hop almost looked like the beefy fellow she had married twenty years ago. Without her glasses his bulk could be mistaken for muscle and the gray stubble on his jaw was invisible. No mistaking the bald head though. "Hop, why don't you get one of them two-pays?"

Hop didn't have time to answer because his rod suddenly took a nose dive into the water. He grabbed it and started cranking in the line. "Get the landing net, Willie Fay." He stood up in the boat and tried to see down through the green water. "Hurry up."

Slow to react, Willie Fay balanced her tea on the seat and inched toward the net. By the time she got it from under the pile of cushions and jackets Hop was holding on to his rod for dear life. "Is it a fish?" she asked.

"Of course it's a fish." Hop knelt in the bottom of the boat and managed to raise the tip of the rod out of the water.

Willie Fay put her glasses on and peered into the water. "Looks more like a big old roasting pan. With legs."

For a brief instant Hop levered his catch into plain view. "It's a damn turtle. I've hooked the edge of his shell." He saw that Willie Fay had the net poised at the side of the boat, so he maneuvered the huge creature toward the boat. "Jeez, it's a snapper." The turtle gave a convulsive shake and jerked the pole from Hop's grasp. Pole, reel, and turtle fell back into the water and knocked the landing net from Willie Fay's hands on the way down.

Willie Fay let out an Amazon sized scream when the turtle plunged through her net. Even Hop, who was used to his wife's proclivity for theatrics, thought she had been mortally wounded. He forgot his fast sinking rod and landing net and scrambled over the middle seat to examine the screaming woman. The boat rocked wildly in the water. He put his arms around her and pulled her close. "Take it easy, Babe, easy." He continued the soothing patter until he got her to sit down. Willie Fay abruptly gave up her screaming and leaned her face against Hop's chest. "I broke a nail." She held her ragged hand in Hop's face so he could see the damage. "I wanna go home."

Of course the red boat got a deep gouge along one side as Hop and Willie Fay dragged it onto the trailer. And of course the transmission went out in the pickup when they crested the steep slope onto the blacktop and they had to call a wrecker to get truck, boat, and trailer home again. And of course Hop had to tell his wife about the time payments and the sad fact that the boat cost several thousand dollars more than he had planned for. And of course Willie Fay had to give Hop the cold shoulder for several weeks as payment for his dumb decision. Then she relented and told him he could use her Buick to tow the boat as long as he took the hitch off when he brought the boat home because she couldn't be expected to put up with the ugly thing when she drove the pink car to the supermarket. And of course they kissed and made up and Hop paid a co-worker a big premium for a half sheet of Elvis stamps which he presented to Willie Fay on her birthday.

And spring limped into summer and summer into

fall. Hop took the boat out three or four times, but the routine of putting the hitch on the pink Buick for the haul to the water, getting the boat launched alone, then reversing the whole process became a chore Hop hadn't bargained on. When the first winter storm threatened, he bought a plastic tarp and wrapped up the boat for the season. It wasn't until he oiled the hitch and put it on a back shelf of the garage that the load of guilt finally left him. He felt so good he took Willie Fay out to eat at Nora's Eat and Save. It was eat till you drop night, so they had a fine old time. The next morning he pulled the red boat out to the road, uncovered it and placed a for sale sign on its windshield. That was the second happiest day of Hop's life.

~~~~

'The Two Happiest Days' grew from a small seed in a newspaper editorial. A writer asked the question 'What are the two happiest days in a man's life' in an attempt to start a discussion. The phrase stuck and grew into this story. Our street was littered with boats on trailers that had probably touched water once or twice in their careers. The couple in the story were modeled from friends of my 'kissing' aunt.

~~~~

THE AUCTION

LAINEY: Priscilla, and I arrive in the stable yard together. It's so early the horses are still in the far pasture, where the dew is rising like grave-yard mist. Mrs. Olden usually has her hired hand bring the boarder horses in for their corn by eight. Pris parks her ancient station wagon next to the fence. The summer heat brings out a sheen of sweat on her upper lip when we get out of the car. Guess she really had the AC cranked up.

"You go catch the horse, while I wait for Dixie to bring the trailer," she says to me. Her voice sounds strained and breathy, from the heat, maybe, or her excess flab. I wonder why I always get to slog through the wet grass to halter that miserable animal.

"When's Dixie coming?" I rummage through the stuff in the backseat until I find the greasy-stiff nylon halter. I know my reasons for selling Jazzy, but I'm beginning to wonder why Pris is so anxious about it. He's my horse. "When, Pris?" I ask again, but she ignores me. I loop the halter over my shoulder with a last glance to see Pris fussing with her hair. She doesn't look at me, so I walk out to the pasture, picking my way carefully to avoid tripping over the strew of broken harrows, disc blades, and frozen tractor engines hiding in the tall grass. Olden Stables is falling apart, an ancient mess with doors rotted away at the bottoms and sinking beams holding up leaky roofs.

PRIS: Dixie and me lean on the top rail and watch Lainey bring the tall horse across the field into the gravel parking lot. Lainey keeps her eyes on the animal and ignores the two women watching. She calls, "Is the trailer ready?"

"Ready," I say. I flip my car keys into the air and catch them, letting their jingle fill the empty air between us. "Do you have five bucks? Dixie needs it. To get enough gas to get the car back to her dad." Damn, she looks frumpy next to Dixie who stands loose, long-legged, waiting against the side of the gray Lincoln, which is now free of the battered horse trailer it had towed into the stable yard.

"Good grief, Priss, if I had money, would I be selling the horse?" Lainey says. She finally looks at me and I'm surprised by the hostility in her face. What does she have to be mad about, I wonder. I tell Dixie she'll have to wait for her money. She wrenches the car door open and slams out of the parking lot.

"What a creep," I say aloud, too loud for such a still moment.

DIXIE: You all would think them girls could at least be grateful, having a friend like me, especially owing me money and all. Can't imagine why they want to haul that beat up old show horse anywhere. Why, he must be at least twenty years old.

LAINEY: The roan horse leans his skinny rump on the trailer's butt chain, one rear foot cocked to reveal a clog of straw and manure wedged into the grooves of his hoof. Down the length of that hoof a quarter crack sneaks out below the metal staple someone had used to stop its spread. Farther up, his leg bunches outward unnaturally, a reminder of a poorly treated tendon bow. Maybe the less discerning will see only the long silvery tail, the high set head, the fire in that white-ringed eye. I suppose we shoulda given him a bath, trimmed him up some to show off his better points. Well, it's too late now.

"Help me with this door, Pris," I say. I've got the old bugger into the trailer at last. She's spent the last hour leaning against the shady side of the barn telling me how to get the horse into the trailer and yet, she's the one sweating. I beat the hair out of my eyes and watch the sweat drip off the ends of her bleached blond hair onto her pillowy shoulders.

JAZZY: That damn trailer is in the drive again. I can't believe the way this keeps happening. These jerks think they can push me around, especially the fat jade with the greasy hair. Who does she think she is, anyway? God, my knees hurt today.

PRIS: Dixie's dad thought he might need his trailer today--what a laugh. No sense letting it rot in his shed when I have a good use for it. It's a fine day for an auction, but I hope that little snot, Lainey, doesn't cause any trouble. Guess I'd better tell Mrs. Olden we're taking Jazzy, now. Don't want her charging us for another day's corn.

MRS. OLDEN: I sit at the kitchen window wondering what those girls are up to. You'd think they could pay some of their back feed bill instead of trying to cheat an old woman. Now they're loading that ancient roan gelding, Jazz. Chin in her hands, Mrs. Olden remembers old Jazz. He sure was used to better things, bright lights, the drum of heavy shod hooves on the sawdust ring, bathing and brushing, applause, and the torture of tail sets and long-shanked bits. He bore the gripping knees forcing him this way and that, the white-knuckled hands lifting his head to an artificial beauty. His roan coat flashed with sweat and hairspray and palmed-on lanolin, while his hard sucking breath accentuated the pound of his hooves on the outer rim of the show ring.

Does Jazz miss the years of ribbons and the trophies and applause as much as I do? Jazz Just A Flame II is his registered name. I don't think those girls even know his name. Did those years on the way down pain him? The times when he was placed in the ranks of those who missed the first cut, the shows he missed all together because he was standing in a dark stall having his leg iced to pull the swelling out. The shots he was given to kill the pain so he could go into the ring anyway. The years he spent giving rides to mean fisted grandchildren, the changes in ownership, over and over. It was a shock when he turned up here again, thin as a scarecrow. Now he's going again.

LAINEY: I watch the road run beneath the front of Pris's old Pontiac wagon. The center line dissolves just under the amber Indian on the hood. The car coughs and knocks until she builds up speed, then we sail smoothly except when Jazzy shifts his weight up against one side of the trailer. When he pulls that stunt, we slew sideways until Pris yanks the wheel to compensate. Even with these distractions, I figure we should be in Hartlinberg by noon. Horses sell at one o'clock. It will be good to get caught up on the feed bill, maybe even the rent. I'll miss old Jazz though, like a toothache. I absently rub the fast swelling bruise above my knee. The old bastard is mean, fast, too.

PRISS: When Lainey told me she was selling Jazzy, I worried she would leave me out. Say the money I gave her was just a loan, not part payment on the horse, but she didn't. I wish I could have got him before his leg went bad. What a team we would have made on the show circuit. We'd have been up to our necks in ribbons and trophies. I'm going to buy a good young horse at the auction, maybe find a real bargain, but right now I need a little pick-me-up.

LAINEY: "What're we stopping for?" I say. Pris has the blinker on and we're slowing down.

"I need to pee. Won't take a minute."

"See that it don't," I say. She pulls up beside a Gas-N-Go.

"Come in with me," she says. "I might need you to hold the door." We get out and Pris locks the car. I can hear Jazzy methodically kicking the back of the trailer as if he had an old grudge against Dixie's father.

RALPH BEARD: These two women come in while I'm refilling the pop cooler. I mostly notice them cause they're arguing. The skinny bitch with ratty brown hair is shrilling at the fat dame. Somethin about money and bein in a rush to get to Hartlinberg. Miss Pudge gets herself a six-pack of tall cold ones out of the cooler, while her friend yaps at her like one of them lap dogs. Gawd, I'd a popped her one.

The skinny one pays, though, with a twenty. They get gone and I figure I'm shed of them, until the fat one comes barreling back all in a lather. She's yapping about her car keys. I tell her not to get her panties in a knot; we search the counter, start on the floor, when the skinny bitch comes in. She says, "The keys are in the car, you duffus. You locked the keys in the car." Oh, man, how many times I seen a dame pull that dumb stunt. I get my coat hanger from behind the counter.

LAINEY: The last sign read forty miles to Hartlinberg. Even pushing this rig to the max means getting there no earlier than one o'clock. The empty beer cans are rattling around in the back seat. Old Jazz has stopped kicking. I expect he's hanging on for dear life, bracing himself on every corner. Pris is hunting a restroom. I can tell by the way she sits up straight, all business, biting her lower lip, clenching and unclenching her thighs. The white-knuckle grip she has on the wheel is another clue.

I just sit and wait and hope she can hold out until Hartlinberg. Finally Priss asks me, "You remember a gas station between Grayson and Hartlinberg?" I tell her, "No." She slows down with an eye out for a side road. We haul off the blacktop onto a frontage track, much too fast. The trailer slides dangerously sideways, almost jack knifing, then rights itself. We bump along this gravel road for a mile or so, then she yanks the rig onto a dirt road that seems to head for a grove of trees.

"Are you sure we should drive down here?" I say. The road looks soft, muddy-like.

"Don't sweat it, Lainey. You worry too much," she

tells me. She stomps the brakes too quickly. The car swerves off the road into the mud.

"Somebody needs to worry," I say. I look over at Pris, see the thin film of sweat on her face, see the quiver of her lower lip, the twitch along her right eye.

"The bottom feels solid. I'll just gun the engine a little and we'll shoot right out of here."

KARLSON: Damn broad shows up at my door wanting me to fire up the tractor to pull her damn car out of the mud. Offers me five dollars. Good Lord, these idiots think they can buy anything. Five dollars and for that she expects me to get up from my lunch and walk clear to the barn, take the mower off the tractor, gas it up , and drive clear to Hell to pull her car out of the mud. I get there and find there's two women and a horse trailer besides. The horse is squalling and sweating like a stuck pig. I tell them they have to unload the horse before I can haul their ass out of the mud. The skinny one finally wades out through the mud and opens the trailer's end gate, but she can't get the horse out. The dumb brute lays over on her every time she tries to push past him to get to his head to untie him. I give up and unload the horse myself. I tie the ugly stick to a tree, then hook to the car and pull it out to the frontage road. Figure I don't want to do the job twice.

PRIS: I didn't realize the auction house parking lot would

be so crowded. Guess that means there are a lot of buyers and sellers here today. If I can just find a place to plant this outfit, we can get the show on the road. I say to Lainey, "I'll stop here, so you can unload Jazzy. I'll have to park down along the road where there's no place to unload." She makes a big fuss about having to do all the work, so I get out to help.

I hadn't realized how much mud Jazzy had picked up back there. Looks like he's wearing hip waders. People are certainly looking at him though. Guess they know a classy animal when they see one. Wonder why Lainey is limping. Boy, does she look funny with all that mud. Good thing I had an old towel for her to sit on or my car would need a steam cleaning.

"Let's tie Jazzy to the fence. You can get the paperwork, while I park the car."

LAINEY: I don't believe it. We can't take Jazzy into the sale barn because we don't have a health certificate. Pris goes to argue with the man, so I'm stuck here in the hot sun with the horse. He's getting tucked up in the flank. I figured we'd have him bedded down in a stall with hay and water by now. We should be getting him cleaned up and ready to go through the auction, but here we sit in the parking lot.

JAKE SMITH: "I'm very sorry Miss, but you need a health certificate issued by a veterinarian before you can bring a horse into the auction barn."

"We've driven all morning. Can't you make an exception?"

"Sorry. There's been shipping fever going around and I can't take a chance."

PRIS: I can't believe the arrogance of these people. They put that stuff about the health papers in fine print at the bottom of the flyer. Well, I'm not going to do business with them again. Some good looking stock here. Guess I might as well look around since we're here.

"Come on, Lainey. Take Jazzy to the trailer." I start walking down the gravel road toward the car thinking Lainey is behind me with Jazzy in tow. When I stop at the car and turn around, she's still half-mile away. What's wrong with that girl, anyway? We don't have all day. The best horses will be sold before I get a chance to look at them.

LAINEY: Shape up Jazzy. Pris says I got to take you back to the trailer. Where does she get off telling me what to do, anyway? Get you tied up snug, then I'm going to get something to eat. Miss Pris can do the horse trading. She can get you a bucket of water, too. I'm going to eat.

SAM TORREY: A couple of pigeons I think when these two women stroll through the barn eye-balling the horses. The scrawny one is stuffin a foot-long into her mouth as fast as she can swallow. The bleached blond looks like she's already stuffed a few too many burgers and shakes in her time. Big talker, too. Non-stop, just like my old lady. She pops a look at my red chestnut saddlebred, so I slip into the stall and give the horse a goose with my pocket prod. A little lectricity really peps them up. That ol red horse sashays back and forth across the stall with his head up real purty-like. I kin tell the fat one's impressed by the way she elbows her friend. My lucky day, she's stoppin to ask about him. If I'm right about this bitch, she'll never touch Red's legs, just go gaga over his purty face and white sox.

PRIS: Try to act like you're not interested, I say to myself. "How much are you asking for this one?" I have a hundred bucks socked away and Lainey must have a few dollars beside Jazzy.

"You can't be serious, Pris. We're supposed to be selling a horse, not buying one."

"Four hundred dollars, Miss," says this guy with yellow teeth and a long droopy mustache. "He's a bargain at that. I'm wanting to get home before dark, so I'm willing to take a beating."

Just when I'm getting down to some serious haggling, Lainey says she'll be back in a minute and goes hobbling off in the direction of the rest rooms.

LAINEY: Gawd what a place to get the trots. I get back to

the barn and there's Pris up on that red horse, bouncing her fat rump on his kidneys and grinning like a monkey. Bet she thinks she looks like a blue ribbon rider up there. The horse looks good, though, flashy and high headed with a long, long tail floating out behind. She hollers at me to check the horse for lameness as she works him up and down the alleyway. He looks okay to me. I wonder where she think she's going to get four hundred bucks, but maybe she's been holding out on me.

SAM TORREY: Red is movin sweet today. That shot of Bute really did the trick, but he won't be able to walk tomorrow after this workout. She sure is a chunk.

PRISS: "You little shit, what do you mean you won't let Torrey have Jazz?" Here I've gone and bargained him down to two seventy five with Jazzy to make up the boot, and Lainey gets stubborn on me. She expects me to haul that horse of hers home again. "Look, I'm goin to sell this red horse as soon as I get him home. Mrs. Olden will probably snap him up. She's a sucker for these show horses. For her granddaughter. Didn't she say her granddaughter was coming for the summer?"

"Maybe. I got to hit the restroom again. We'll talk about it."

SAM TORREY: She fell head over heels for my old red horse, hook, line and sinker. Says she don't have four hundred bucks, but she can lay a Franklin on me if I take a check and another horse for the rest.

"You'll have to walk down the road a ways, if you want to see him," she says. "We have to wait for Lainey to get back."

"No problem," I say. I give the red horse a good rub down to keep him nice and shiny. Wish I could give him another shot of Bute. Don't want the merchandise gimping around on three legs before the deals is shook.

LAINEY: "We'll be in Grayson in a few minutes," I say to Pris. "Stop at the Enco station." I don't need to worry about her arguing with me at least. Sure hope Sam Torrey don't cash that check before Wednesday.

When I get out to use the restroom, I check on the red horse in the trailer. "He's been awful quiet," I say to Pris. "Standing hip-shot, too." I look at the horse's right rear leg resting on the point of its shoe on the trailer floorboards. It looks swollen, filled through the whole tendon area.

"He's not a trailer climber like that damn Jazzy, just relaxed. It's nice to haul a horse that knows how to behave," answers Pris.

SAM TORREY: Couldn't believe the horse those two dames had tied to their trailer. Muddy and unclipped, but tall and big boned. Little smart asses thought I wouldn't notice the bowed tendon under all the mud. Or the fact that their pony is mighty long in the tooth. I humor them by ignoring it. The only thing that matters is how much the animal weighs. This one will cross the scales at well over a thousand pounds. Even at a quarter a pound I make out like a bandit.

~~~~

The characters in the 'The Auction' are closer to home. I bought the old roan show horse for $20. A friend had begged me to buy Laddie [Jazzy] to save him from slaughter one fall in the late 1960's. We had not moved to the country yet and I had to spring for the old horse's board as well. Another friend, Pris, finally hauled him to her place in the country where Laddie spent the winter finding ways to get out of his pasture. The post master in a nearby town brought him home one time, a patrolman another. Often a phone call or a message demanding we come get our horse interrupted my day. By spring I knew we had to take drastic steps. Laddie had to go. The trip and the horse sale in Harrisburg happened just about the way I wrote it. Sometimes it is hard to tell truth from fiction. Horse sales and animal rescues—never again. Pris did buy the flashy horse from the dealer, but the poor animal was not up packing her weight and soon went totally lame. A local veterinarian advised her to give the animal a big shot of bute and haul him to an auction far from home. She refused and nursed him back to some semblance of health. She rode him at a slow walk on the back county roads for several months before he fell and fractured his shoulder. No healing from that so he was put down.

~~~~

The Grape-Eyed Cat

Carrie and Hannah

Hannah leaned back against the red Mustang and squinted up at Watt Hill. Green with the fresh leaves of spring, the sandstone ridge merged into the Big Muddy River bottom in a series of broken ledges. Tulip poplar, sweetgum, and sassafras sprouted from every patch of soil. The small house snugged against the base of the hill, almost invisible with its bark-gray siding and rusted tin roof.

"The house looks smaller," said Hannah. She walked through the long grass to the front door.

Jogging to keep up, the lawyer produced a Yale key on a frayed pink ribbon. "Probably been awhile since you've been here." He unlocked the door and handed Hannah the key.

"Yes, more than thirty-five years." She put the key in her jeans pocket. "Has this house been painted since the war?"

"Which war would that be Miss Anderson?" The lawyer juggled his frayed portfolio and wiped his forehead with a ratty handkerchief.

"Which war? Any war. What difference does it

make," said Hannah. "This place looks like a fishing camp."

"Sorry about that," said the lawyer. He wadded his handkerchief into the back pocket of his suit pants. "It's hard to get anyone to come out here to clean and paint."

"You drew a salary from the estate for upkeep as well as legal matters." Hannah turned to face the sweaty, little man. "I'd like an accounting of all expenditures."

"If you sign these transfer papers, the Brasskamp estate is all yours." The lawyer looked up at her. "The place is a mess, but at least there's no mortgage."

"What are these lien papers then?" She took a step towards him and pulled a couple of red stamped documents from the pile the lawyer held out to her.

"Tax liens. I'm afraid old Carrie neglected her property tax obligations the last few years." The lawyer ran his stubby finger around the inside of his collar.

"Last quite a few years it looks like." Hannah scowled down at the lawyer's balding head. "It's a wonder the county didn't put the property in the tax sale."

"Well, maybe they figured the place would revert to the state anyway. No one expected an heir to show up." He fiddled with the button that strained to hold his shirt closed across a budding paunch. "I know Randall Adams has his eye on the land. He owns the farm over the ridge."

"Thanks for your help." She ran her fingers through her short cropped hair. "I'll come by your office and pick up that list of expenditures."

"Randall will buy you out," countered the lawyer. "It's probably the best thing you can do."

"Do you sell real estate on the side?" She walked him to his faded Buick. "Or is Randall Adams your brother-in -law?"

"Cousin." The old Buick sagged with his weight. "I doubt if land prices will hold at this level past the new year."

"Nonsense," she said. "Land is always a good investment."

"It's going to take a lot of money to get this place in shape." The lawyer cranked the complaining side-window part-way down. "Better to sell than to throw good money after bad."

"I don't think so." She stepped back when the lawyer put the Buick in reverse and clunked out the driveway.

Retracing her steps to the house, Hannah wondered about the wisdom of uprooting herself and moving to Southern Illinois. Must be something in our genes, she said to herself, remembering that Great Aunt Carrie had made a similar move to this remote place sixty years ago.

Carrie A. Hanson stood on the railway platform

with her paisley carpet bag and brass bound trunks. "Excuse me," she said to the railroad yard man. He stopped loading strawberry flats onto the express to Chicago and turned to the tall woman in the flowered picture hat.

"Yes maam?"

"Is the city of Carbondale nearby?" Carrie asked. "And may I hire a conveyance for myself and my baggage?"

"I'm afraid you're looking at our fine city, what there is of it." He pushed his blue cap back on his head. "Shank's mare is the usual transportation. Most folks live here or have someone meeting them."

"Jake would be meeting me, but I'm a day early." She fanned herself with a letter.

"That wouldn't be Jimmie Jake Bessler now?" asked the man. "He'll be down at the pool hall this time a day."

"Why, yes. That's the name." Her gray eyes glittered behind steel-rimmed spectacles. "Pool hall? What's a man doing in a pool hall at ten in the morning?"

"It's about the only time he can get shed of the younguns." The man left his strawberry flats and stopped a railroad conductor who had just stepped off the train. "Sir, this lady may be needing some assistance."

"Younguns, children, are you saying Jimmie Jake has children?" He doesn't mention any children in this letter."

"We meet again." The conductor swept off his hat and bowed over Carrie's hand. "Let me introduce myself this time. I'm Wilbur Brasskamp."

"And I'm Miss Carrie Hanson." She turned to the yard man who had forgotten about his strawberries. "Thank you very much for your help."

"You have business with Mr. Bessler?" Mr. Brasskamp asked.

"Business, yes. I came to marry him." Carrie showed Mr. Brasskamp the letter and a contract. "He sent me money for the train fare."

"Make yourself comfortable in the station waiting room, while I have someone put these trunks in the check room." Wilbur Brasskamp cleared his throat and exchanged glances with the yard man. "Then we'll see about Mr. Jimmie Jake Bessler."

Carrie waited nervously for her husband-to-be. She re-read the letters and contract for the hundredth time. Was she crazy to agree to marry someone sight-unseen? Maybe Brother Charlie was right. She could have gone with him to homestead on the barren plains of South Dakota when the family home in Boston sold to settle the estate. Children? Did someone say that Jimmie Jake had children? She supposed she could learn to care for a couple of children. Why didn't he mention them to her? Get a hold of yourself there, Carrie, she told herself firmly.

The clatter of footsteps roused Carrie from her private thoughts. The waiting room seemed to fill with children of all sizes. Lank, rough-cut, white-blond hair, bare feet, and narrow-set blue eyes marked boys and girls alike.

"Line up and introduce yourselves to your new ma," chirruped a scrawny fellow. A scant hand taller than the biggest child, Jimmie Jake Bessler marshaled the children into a ragged line.

"Thelma June." The tallest child twisted her skimpy pigtails nervously.

"Jimmie Bob," said a reed-thin boy with a black eye and scabby knees.

"Eddie Bob, here." He wiped his nose on his sleeve. "You coming home with us?"

"Louisa Jane, madam." She tripped over her too-long skirt and punched the younger girl pressed up beside her.

"I'm Matilda Jane," shrieked sister number three. "I'll get you for that, Louisa."

"Lucinda Jane." Invisible behind the bigger kids, number four seemed bewildered when she was thrust to the front of the group.

"Hilda, here," said another small girl with hair cut short as her brothers.

"Jake. I'm Jake, not Joey. That's Joey. He's real stupid." Jake grinned like a fiend.

"I'm Joey and I don't want no new ma." He turned

and buried his face in his sister's skirt.

"Me Buddy." The red cheeked toddler sat down on the dirty floor and started crying.

"Now, Thelma June, get these younguns back to school," said Jimmie Jake. "No fooling around. Just march, straight to school."

Speechless, Carrie watched the mob of children troop out of the station, punching, kicking, and pulling each other's hair.

"I've got everything arranged with the justice of the peace." Jimmie Jake's lopsided grin showed his gap-spaced, tobacco stained teeth. "Let's go."

"Just a minute Mr. Bessler." Carrie stood up and unfolded the letter she held. "I believe we have something to discuss."

"Lordy, you're a tall one." Jimmie Jake squinted up at her, moving his chaw of Old Red from one side to the other. "I hope you have a ring. Something came up and I had to hock Junie's ring."

"Mr. Bessler, about this photograph you sent of yourself." Carrie held the picture out for the growing audience to see. "This can't possibly be you."

"Oh that." Jimmie Jake shot a mouthful of tobacco juice into the nearest spittoon. "I borrowed it from Merle Becker over at the Post Office."

"How many children do you have?" Carrie had to raise her voice to be heard over the laughter of the crowd. "You certainly didn't mention them."

"They say ten's no more work than one." He reached for her arm. "They take care of each other. "Let's go, woman."

"Mr. Bessler, though I'm a good Lutheran woman, I'd rather enter a nunnery than marry you." Carrie plucked Jimmie Jake's hand from her sleeve and wiped her fingers on a lace hanky. The crowd roared with laughter when Carrie dropped the hanky into the nearby trash can. Like Moses parting the waters, she strode through the crowded waiting room to the station platform. Jimmie Jake Bessler and Wilbur Brasskamp followed her outside.

"You can't do this to me." Jimmie Jake's adam's apple bobbed frantically. "I have my rights."

"Shut up, fool." Wilbur touched Carrie's elbow protectively. "You'll need a place to stay. The next train north isn't until tomorrow."

"Thank you." Carrie let him take her carpet bag.

"Sara Meecher runs the boarding house." Wilbur offered his arm to Carrie as they descended the platform steps to the street. "It's clean and cheap. Sara's a good person."

"I'm sure it will be just fine."

But it wasn't 'just fine' thought Hannah. She remembered sitting on the rose and green Aubausson carpet listening to Carrie recount events at Sara Meecher's boarding house. "I wonder if that carpet is still in the parlor?" The yellow-eyed tom cat on the front step didn't answer. Hannah walked into the quiet house, into an envelope of musty, mousy air.

The living room was solid with stacks of junk, bisected with open paths to the kitchen, bathroom, bedroom, and back door. Folded and flattened Cheerios boxes, bundles of feed sacks, government publications, many still in their familiar brown envelopes, and boxes of Mason jars, filled every empty space in the small house. The parlor door, blocked by a pile of newspapers reaching the ceiling, guarded long forgotten secrets.

"Do you ever have your work cut out for yourself," Hannah said to herself. "Maybe I can hire someone in the neighborhood to help me."

After several days of hard work, the two women had cleared the debris of years of frugal living from the house.

"Now I need to get someone to haul this heap of trash to the landfill," said Hannah.

"My grandson, Davy, can do it for you," said Liddy. "He's got him a long-bed pickup with racks."

"Thanks. I really appreciate your help." Hannah carried a last bale of old newspapers to the pile by the driveway. "Now I can see what the house is really like."

"Well, we can sure use the extra money." Liddy added a heavy box of rusted plumbing fixtures to the pile. "Your Carrie wasn't much of a housekeeper, especially after Wilbur died. She sewed some mighty handsome coats and dresses though. Folks came from as far away as Cape Giarado for fittings."

"I knew she made quilts for the orphanage at Harrisburg, but I never knew Carrie was a dressmaker." Hannah plucked a tiger-stripped kitten from the pile of boxes. "Was she having financial problems?"

"Oh, no, Miss Hannah. She was the saving sort, but she always helped out where it was needed." Liddy followed Hannah back inside. "When the Jackson family was burned out, she bought them a cook stove and a full tank of propane for their new home. And she gave my Davy eighty dollars for the insurance and registration on his first car."

"Carrie didn't pay her property taxes the last few years. Do you know anything about that?" Hannah poured two glasses of ice tea and sat down at the kitchen table. "Rest awhile, Liddy."

"Don't sound right to me." Liddy traced figures in the condensation on the tea glass. "Barney Jones would come by and pick up her money and pay her taxes the same time as he paid his own."

"Guess I'll get the chance to talk to Mr. Jones soon." Hannah concealed her surprise from Liddy. "Thanks for helping me."

"Sure you won't be needing anything else?" Liddy pocketed the money Hannah counted out. "I could wash the windows and mop."

"Maybe later," said Hannah. "For now, just send Davy around with his truck."

After Liddy had gone, Hannah unlocked the parlor door . Except for a layer of dust and a few spider webs, the rose and green patterned carpet looked bright and new.   Hannah sank down on the soft rug, trying to remember every word that Carrie had said to her that long ago evening.

Breakfast at Sara Meecher's boarding house was noisy and informal. An assorted group, men and women, waited around the long table, waited for one of Sara Meecher's home-cooked breakfasts.

"Been to this area before, Miss Hanson?" The portly man flipped his derby hat onto the coat rack and sat down.

"No. I lived in Boston the past five years and in Indiana before that." Carrie unfolded her napkin and spread it on her lap. "Do you stay here often?"

"I sell farm machinery parts. You know, harrow tines, mower bars and teeth, belts, blades." The salesman tucked his napkin into the neck of his collarless shirt. "Best grub in all of Illinois here."

"You the one Jimmie Jake Bessler sweet-talked into coming out here to wife him?" A prim, neat woman in blue took the chair next to Carrie. "Wonder when he's going to learn."

"You're the third one, so far." Sara Meecher

unloaded her tray of heavy serving platters. "That we know of that is."

"The man should be in jail." Carrie looked at the steaming platter of force meat and bacon, then passed it to the salesman, who forked off a half a dozen sausages and a wad of bacon.

"Can't blame the man for wanting someone to tend that flock of children." The salesman reached for the egg plate and helped himself to a generous serving. "What do you think, Sister Ina?"

"Now, Calvin, you know how I feel." The plump, florid woman took two biscuits and passed the basket to her neighbor. "Those younguns should've been sent to the orphanage at Harrisburg three year ago, when their ma died of the fever. They've become a bunch of wild animals."

"Better have some of this white gravy for your biscuits, Miss Hanson."

"Got to keep your strength up."

"Fresh pot of coffee coming up." Sara Meecher placed the blue enamel pot and a jug of fresh cream in the center of the table.

"Miss Hanson, there's someone to see you." A straw-haired boy stuck his head in the dining room door. "Deputy sheriff, I think."

"I wonder what he wants." Carrie Hanson dropped her napkin on her chair and hurried to the parlor. "Sheriff, what can I do for you?"

"Miss Carrie Hanson?" The deputy handed her a long, white envelope. "You're required to appear before Magistrate Hill at 2:00 p.m. today."

"You're serving me a summons?" Carrie held the envelope by one corner, much as one might hold a dead mouse. "Jimmie Jake Bessler's work?"

"Yes maam." The deputy picked up his hat and headed for the door. "Sorry about interrupting your breakfast."

Carrie returned to Sara Meecher's table to finish her meal. She couldn't help feeling anxious about the summons, but other questions loomed bigger in her mind. She must make some important decisions before her money ran out.

By year's end Carrie Hanson became Carrie Brasskamp. She and Wilbur moved into a snug farm house on the Big Muddy River. The land had originally been granted to a returning veteran of the Civil War, a Major Zedadiah Hill. Zedadiah's failed attempt at farming those 140 acres of bottom land and thicket was chalked up to his inexperience and shell shock. Foreclosure followed foreclosure on the Big Muddy farm. The abstract for the property was as thick as a man's forearm when the Brasskamps bought the farm from the Bank of Gorham.

With a steady salary from the railroad and no intention of farming, Wilbur and Carrie paid the place off.

The bank tried to persuade them to mortgage and build a bigger house. They refused, saying the house was quite big enough for the two of them, thank you.

Because of his job, Wilbur was home only a few days every fortnight. This suited Carrie just fine. She read mountains of books and newspapers provided by the new state library system. She studied government booklets on canning green beans, raising angora rabbits, and the how to's of building a brooder house. Once Carrie became proficient in putting up bread 'n butter pickles, spiced crab apples, and tomato relish, she took up volunteer work to fill her days. She learned to make bright crazy quilts and strange little books whose every page was filled solid with pictures cut from discarded magazines and greeting cards. Quilts and books were given to the children at the county hospital and orphanage. When Carrie learned of the birth of her grand-niece, Hannah, she wrapped up her latest crazy quilt and an extra scrap book and mailed them to her.

Every two weeks, when Wilbur drew his railroad pay, he stopped at the City Bank in Murphysboro. On alternate pay days he would make a deposit in a savings account. The other paydays he traded a crisp twenty dollar bill for a mint twenty dollar gold piece. This double eagle he brought home to Carrie, along with a rose or a bright handkerchief. Carrie carefully wrapped the coins in cotton muslin and put them away.

The year Hannah turned eleven, Wilbur had his first

heart attack. When he was up and around again, Hannah's parents decided it was time to visit the Brasskamps. Hannah remembered one particularly heated conversation.

"What do you think about that Roosevelt?" asked Wilbur.

"Aah! The New Deal." answered Hannah's father. "He'll probably bankrupt the country, if he's elected."

"Well, things can't get much worse than they are right now," said Carrie.

"No jobs, long bread lines, banks failing," said Wilbur.

"We're lucky though. No black dust blizzards here," said Carrie. "And the corn is doing good this year."

"What about the rumor that Roosevelt will take us off the gold standard?" asked Hannah's father.

"And make owning gold against the law," said Hannah's mother.

"He's promised a program to bring electricity to country folks like us," said Wilbur.

"And a job core to put people to work," said Carrie. "We've heard about a plan to build a lodge over by Makanda. On those hardacre farms the government bought out."

"Handouts." said Hannah's father. "It just means more taxes and more debt."

"At least Hoover will keep the budget balanced," said Hannah's mother.

"People need relief now." said Wilbur. "They can't wait for that 'do nothing' president."

"Hannah, why don't you and I go do something interesting," said Carrie. "And leave these folks to their politicking."

Carrie steered Hannah into the parlor, a room dwarfed by tall bookcases and a glass-fronted china cabinet. Sitting together on the Auboisson carpet, Carrie and Hannah poked through a box of carved beads and black jet buttons. Then Hannah helped Carrie sort and mount a pile of picture post cards in an album. They cut and pasted flowers, dogs, and smiling children into a book for the orphanage. Finally Carrie unlocked a mahogany cabinet with a small key she wore on a chain around her neck.

"Just a peek here," she said to Hannah. "Its past your bed time."

"Oh. Money," said Hannah. "I have a collection of buffalo nickels, Auntie."

"These are twenty dollar gold pieces," said Carrie. "Most folks call them double eagles."

"What will happen to them if the government decides it owns all the gold?" asked Hannah.

"Goodness sakes, child," said Carrie. "I'm surprised you understood all that talk."

"They're very beautiful," said Hannah. "Especially the Saint-Gaudens."

"Where did you learn about Saint-Gaudens?"

asked Carrie.

"Augustus Saint-Gaudens," said Hannah. "We studied him in art class. Miss Henderson said he was one of America's greatest modern sculptors."

"Well, there won't be any more double eagles. The bank hasn't had them for months. Someone said the government melted down all the 1933 gold coins," said Carrie. "Here, let me show you something really special."

Working through stacks of old newspapers, carefully folded and flattened Cheerios boxes, bundles of feed sacks, government publications, and boxes of fruit jars, Hannah realized the rubbish and neglect were only a patina, a thin layer frosting the trim, snug house she remembered. The closets, cupboards, and storage areas were neat and orderly. The house itself was sound under its peeling paint and flapping screens. Its sills, doors, and roof still capable of keeping out weather and varmints. Hard work, paint, and nails would go a long way.

When the deadline for paying the back taxes approached, Hannah began searching for Aunt Carrie's coin collection. In particular, Hannah wanted to find the gold double eagles. Carrie's safety deposit box had been crammed full of stuff. The deed to the house and 140 acres, a $50 war bond worth far more as a collectors item, dozens of proof sets and type coins, but no $20 gold. Hannah found a 1909-S, V.D.B. cent in almost mint condition and a complete set of Indian Head pennies in the lock box. Both were very rare and valuable, but nothing compared to the 1907 Saint-Gaudens with Roman numerals and wire rim Carrie had showed her years ago.

That one beautiful, high relief coin was worth more than the house, the land, and all the rest of Aunt Carrie's estate combined. Hannah wondered if she could bear to part with it when she found it. If she found it, she corrected herself.

Hannah continued going through the piles and boxes in the storage area under the eaves of the mute house. Sorting through a lifetime of jigsaw puzzles, Christmas ornaments, ribbon-tied bundles of letters, and endless mounds of books, Hannah suffered niggling pangs of doubt. Shoulders aching and stomach growling, she slumped down on the tar paper floor to rest. Maybe she was wrong about seeing the rare coin or maybe Carrie had sold it years ago.

The squall of a cat cut through Hannah's thoughts. Jerking around, she saw a black cat perched on a stack of old phone books. She didn't recognize this cat with his boiled-grape eyes. All of Carrie's cats had yellow eyes and how did this black puss get into the house?

The cat eluded Hannah's quick grab and knocked over the dusty pile of directories with his powerful leap. Over-balanced, Hannah sprawled face down in the middle of the mess. When she moved to get up, she noticed a sheet of lined notebook paper taped inside one of the phone books. Easing the Carbondale-Murphysboro Area Directory 1961 from the jumble, Hannah found a diagram and a sketchy map. Clearly labeled across the bottom of the map was Big Muddy River. A rectangle above it was surely the pole barn and a small square, the tool shed.

Racing out to the barn, Hannah searched for the cast off telephone pole supporting a section of the roof. From there she found the broken concrete water tank marked on the diagram and soon located the two spots indicated by Xs. Finding a rusty shovel, she began to dig, scattering dirt everywhere. When the sun slid below the willow trees, she uncovered a faded red coffee can taped shut with silver duct tape. Singing and giggling, she lugged the heavy can to the house. After cutting through the layers of tape with an old skinning knife, she finally dumped its contents on the table. It was coins all right, Liberty Bell halves, walking liberty halves, buffalo nickels, and Morgan dollars. But no gold.

Giving up, Hannah staggered off to bed. The grape-eyed cat joined her, running from X to X, pawing through layer after layer of yellow clay to reveal another faded red can. Each can seemed to be the promised one, but each rusted and crumbled away at her touch.

When Hannah opened her eyes at first light, the black cat was sitting beside her, waiting. Together they trotted to the barn to search again.

The other X yielded another red can. This one held

only pennies. Sitting on the mound of dirt wondering what to do next, Hannah watched a white Ford pickup rattle up the driveway.

"Great. Just what we need, company," said Hannah. She turned to the cat, but it had vanished.

"Hello. I'm Randle Adams."

"And I suppose you're here to rescue me from my plight," retorted Hannah. She didn't bother to stand up.

"Just thought I'd introduce myself. My farm borders the back of your place."

"The knight in shining armor with his white horse, no, white truck, to the rescue," said Hannah. She studied his muddy work boots carefully.

"I'm not too partial to rescuing maidens with straw in their hair and mud on their faces, so you needn't worry," answered Randle. "Actually, I'm here to ask your permission to retrieve a lost cow that scrambled through the fence into your river bottom field."

"Whatever," said Hannah. The knight was too short and skinny.

"Does that mean yes?" asked Randle.

"Why not," said Hannah.

"What are you digging anyway?" asked Randle. "Oh. I know. The family gold."

"I'm planting geraniums," said Hannah.

"Every family in the county has some story about lost gold or a cache of silver dollars," said Randle. "My Uncle Clarence put his in the well."

"Go find your cow."

"How about I help you dig."

"Did you ever find your uncle's gold?"

"What? No, of course not," said Randle absently. "Guess I'd better get my cow."

When the white truck bumped out of sight, the black cat returned to the first hole, purring. While the cat snooped at the bottom of the hole, Hannah fetched the shovel. One foot, then two. When she gave up and stopped, the cat scratched the hard earth and meowed. With one last shove, Hannah heard the grate of metal on metal. Another faded red can. She sat down hard on the mound of dirt.

"Is that can supposed to sprout geraniums?"

"What are you doing here?" said Hannah. She clutched the can close, trying to hide it. The cat tried to claw himself into her lap.

"Where'd you get that witch's cat?" asked Randle. "I don't remember seeing him around here before."

"What do you want?" asked Hannah. She tried to shove the damp hair out of her eyes and disengage from the cat without losing her hold on the can.

"The gate's locked," said Randle. He grinned and reached for the cat.

"Maybe there's a key at the house," said Hannah. She stood up and the cat launched himself at Randle.

"Mean bugger isn't he," said Randle. He stuck his wounded finger in his mouth.

"There's a bunch of keys on a nail in the kitchen. Maybe one of them fits the lock on the gate," said Hannah. She stalked up the worn path to the house, keeping the heavy can pressed close to her dirty shirt.

"Umm, no. I believe the key is in that blue vase," said Randle. He pointed to an earthenware jar on a low shelf in the entryway. "You've cleaned things up. Place looks like it used to, before old Carrie got sick."

"How do you know where the key is?" asked Hannah.

"Sure hope you've found whatever it is you're a hunting," said Randle. "The river is on the rise and it'll cover that barn lot with a couple of foot of water."

"What. The water gets that high?" said Hannah.

"Not every year. But every twenty or thirty years, we get what the experts call a hundred year flood," said Randle. He fished a brass key out of the blue vase. "It looks like this is the year."

"Oh. Great." Hannah continued into the house and plunked the can down on the table.

"Guess I'm back to cow hunting," called Randle. "You sure you can't use a little help with that?"

"Don't forget to lock the gate when you leave," said Hannah.

Alone, Hannah opened the can and poured out a mess of wheat pennies. In the bottom of the can, a handful of square, cloth covered packets remained, wedged in by a small notebook. Unwrapping each packet carefully, Hannah lined up a row of six double eagles on the table.

"All common dates," Hannah said to the cat. "Worth about four hundred dollars each. Not quite enough for the taxes."

Tossing the notebook into the junk drawer, Hannah shuffled off to bed. A sudden crashing noise roused her from a restless sleep a few hours later.

"Must be Randle bringing back the key," she muttered. She slid back over the edge into sleep. The cat woke her up the second time. He had draped himself over her neck like a stone. Hannah fought through the layers of sleep, still digging the hard earth of the barn lot. Hard pounding on the front door brought her up out of the pit. Dragging the cat from her chest, she crawled out of bed. She pulled on a pair of jeans and fumbled with the door latch. She could hear sirens in the distance.

"Barn's on fire, lady," shouted the neighbor boy. "Do you have a hose somewhere?"

"I think I saw one hanging in the carport," said Hannah. "Should I call someone? Fire department or sheriff?"

"Already did. They're on the way," said the kid. "Won't do much good, but maybe they can keep it from spreading to the woods."

At first light, Hannah stood at the edge of the sodden barn lot with a motley group, firemen, neighbors, and curiosity seekers.

"Was there electricity to the barn?" asked the deputy.

"No," said Hannah. She kicked at a pile of wet debris and noticed she was barefoot.

"What was stored there? Any chemicals or fuel?" asked the deputy.

"No," interrupted Randle Adams. "Old Carrie had let me store hay in the barn. We'd used most of it over the winter so there was only about two hundred bales left."

"Expect it was set then," muttered the deputy. He turned to escort the onlookers back to their cars.

"Bubba Fraser's work, no doubt," said Randle. "Can't even see your geranium holes, Hannah."

"Who is Bubba Fraser." said Hannah. "And why would he burn my barn?"

"The local firebug. Nothing personal. He just likes to see things burn."

"Why don't they lock him up?"

"We do, but the do-gooders get him cleaned up, and properly repentant, and he's out again."

"Unbelievable," said Hannah. "Well, thanks for helping. Sorry about your hay."

"I could bring over a tractor and blade to clean up this mess."

"No. Not yet anyway," said Hannah. "Thanks."

"Guess the river will clean it up eventually," said Randle. "At least you found your treasure before all this."

"Only I didn't," said Hannah. Shoulders slumped, she headed for the house.

"What?" He followed her into the kitchen. "You've got to let me help. I'm not the enemy, really."

"I should go back to Rapid City," said Hannah. "You can have this stupid farm."

"What would you do there?" asked Randle. He had noticed the gold coins lined up in the jumble of duct tape, pennies, and red cans on the table.

"Get down on my knees and grovel and hope they give me my old job back," said Hannah She watched him place the gold coins in a neat stack, holding them by their edges.

"What job would that be?"

"I was curator and head of collections at the School of Mines Museum," said Hannah. "Mostly fossils, mineral specimens, and Indian artifacts. The coin and medal collection was getting some recognition though."

"And you think Carrie had something worthy of a museum?" asked Randle. He fingered the wheat pennies.

"Something worthy of the Smithsonian," conceded Hannah. "Soot is very becoming on you."

"Is any of this stuff valuable?" asked Randle. "When did you last take a bath?"

"Oh." shrieked Hannah. She tripped over the grape-eyed cat on her way to the hall mirror. A stranger peered at her from the old looking glass. Her face was black, with pale tear trails down both gaunt cheeks. Her short cropped hair was the same mud-caked brown as the night gown she had worn as a shirt most of the night.

"Oh, gross. The creature from the swamp."

"More like the Big Muddy Monster," said Randle. "Go take a shower. I'll stick around in case the deputy needs anything."

"O.K., thanks," said Hannah. Grabbing up an armload of clean clothes, she disappeared into the bathroom.

When she emerged, Randle had fed the black cat and the smell of coffee filled the house. He looked up from the notebook he was reading. "Much better."

"Where did you find the notebook?" she asked.

"In the drawer. I was looking for the can opener," said Randle. "Pretty interesting. Have you read this yet?"

"No. I guess I tossed it in there last night," said Hannah. "It was in the bottom of the can with the gold."

"If old Carrie's inventory is correct, there should be several hundred of these ducats somewhere," said Randle. He held one of the coins up to his eye, monocle fashion.

"Does she mention one special coin?" asked Hannah.

"I'm not sure," said Randle. "Here, you look."

"Umm, yes, here it is," said Hannah. "But where is this stuff. I've dug up every spot marked on the map."

"You have a map?" asked Randle. Reaching for her hand, he dropped the coin and stepped on the cat's tail.

"It's contagious," laughed Hannah. "Here's the map."

They bent over the map together, trying to match it to clues in the notebook. The cat with the boiled grape eyes sat on the end of the table washing himself.

~~~~

The 'Grape-Eyed Cat' is set in the same Southern Illinois hill country, but several of the elements happened elsewhere. Carrie Hanson Braskamp was my great aunt. She did, indeed, agree to be a mail order bride, but it all played out in Canton. Canton, South Dakota or Canton, Iowa I'm not sure, but her intended husband did have ten children and she did not marry him. Aunt Carrie was an accomplished seamstress and hat maker. Her eventual husband, Mr. John Braskamp, worked for the railroad and they lived happily until his death in 1946.

The legend of the buried gold was a persistent myth in Southern Illinois with occasional small finds to keep it fresh over the years. We saved one pound size Folger's coffee cans to stash pennies, nickels, and silver dimes for later burial against the possibility of total chaos and the shut down of government and banks alike. We were not alone in this endeavor. One family filled fruit jars with silver dollars and sunk them in their well. This was not a fool proof method of saving money. Pennies tended to corrode into worthless, solid masses. Nickels became gunky messes. There was also the problem of retrieving the loot when it was needed or the owner moved to a new property. Carrie's gold seemed to have suffered such a fate. And who knew if she shared this method of saving with her Little Egypt neighbors.

~~~~

FAR AWAY PLACES

Two Worlds

A hot, June wind, armed with gritty dust, blasted a city on the far side of the world. Two women approached from opposite sides of a cluttered sidewalk near the Forbidden City. They had never met before, and after this brief interval, they would not meet again.

Kuoug Soon was small woman, all shuffling feet and flapping sleeves. Her jet hair streaked with white was pulled tight behind her ears in a hard twist. A woven bamboo coolie hat sucked at her head, its chin chord biting at her sunken cheeks. She held a covered bird cage by the silver ring wired to its rusty top. The ancient crone gave no sign that her knobbed, crooked fingers ached as they grasped the slender handle. Her old style Mao suit with its shapeless, faded tunic and loose pajama-like trousers enfolded her spare body. Only her obsidian eyes and crinkled grin contradicted her dusty grayness.

Silvia Shane was smooth and new. A tall, tanned, willowy, young Canadian, she wore gold sandals and a 'little' dress of lime green cotton. Her long, ashy-blond hair fell heavy around her bare shoulders, drawing the attention of sidewalk loungers and quick moving pedestrians alike.

Face-to-face on the cracked, ragged sidewalk, the two women stopped and stared at one-another. Quick as smoke, the old woman held up the bird cage, then whipped off its cover. The tiny bird inside puffed up its blond ruff and burst into song. Enchanted, the tall girl listened with her hands folded, loose and graceful, across her breasts. When the bird finished its song, the old woman replaced the cover and disappeared down a narrow alley of over-hanging tin roofs. The stench of a public toilet mixed with the tang of heating cooking oil at the Dum Sin Restaurant on the corner.

As the old woman disappeared down the alley, a crowd of curious people gathered. One bystander in particular, a Chinese man with a thin goatee caught her eye. The bystander wore a custom suit of pin-stripe serge and mirror-finish wing-tip shoes, perfect, spotless against the background of the street. He gestured to Silvia as soon as he saw that the bird woman had disappeared down the alley. Standing before her on the pavement, he wrung his hands together at chest level, then pretended to eat. He concluded his mock meal by licking his fingers and delicately probing a back tooth for invisible particles.

Silvia stared at the man's antics, not quite

comprehending his meaning. With a frown he swaggered up and down the pavement, thrusting his hips out to pantomime the expected result of eating the songbird with lewd reality. Silvia gasped at this new reality and stumbled back to the hotel, disgusted and diminished.

~~~~

On a visit to the bird market in an alley near the center of Beijing in 1994 I observed a college age girl, American or British, engaged in an attempt to converse with an old lady with a bird cage. Her attempts at conversation were futile and what she did learn was very unwelcome. Tourists and students alike need to tread lightly. There is a seedy side to the pet markets of Beijing and Shanghai and Hong Kong. It did give me the germ of this story.

Most of the bird markets in the far East are devoted to selling birds for pets and food. Also fish, turtles, cats, crickets, spiders, and various other exotic creatures to fill the demand for a curious Chinese habit of walking these animals in the many parks of the city. The more rare and exotic the creature, the better. Preservationists protest these markets because they may decimate some colonies of rare creatures, birds especially.

~~~~

The following three stories also grew out of chance encounters, one in Moscow, one in Florence, the other in Budapest. This is not as fertile a field for ideas as one would think. At least not for me. Travel can be very isolating because of short stays and the overwhelming numbers of languages and dialects in the world. In some places you become invisible, in others you are an object of curiosity. Neither state encourages creative writing.

~~~~

Two Sides of the Coin

The day was bright and strangely cool for August. How far north was Moscow anyway? The pedestrian shopping street, the Arbat, teemed with shoppers, tourists, vendors, and thieves. I strolled cautiously, ignoring the sleeve tugging boys selling cheap pins and fake Red Army medals. Older boys danced in front of me offering T-shirts with Mickey Mouse at the Kremlin and faded slides of the Armory's treasures, all available at the Hotel Ukraina's gift shop for half the price.

Today, I was hunting for more substantial souvenirs. Through a break in the crowd, I noticed an old man seated on a folding stool with a small selection of coins for sale including a fine set of silver kopeks from the reign of the last czar, Nicholas II. The two headed eagles glared fiercely from the reverse of each coin when I asked, "How much?"

"Five dollars." The old man held up five fingers and peered at me with hope in his rheumy eyes.

"Are you sure?" I asked, amazed because the set would cost eighty or ninety dollars in the states.

"Four dollars." Not understanding he held up four

shaking fingers.

From the medals on his worn gray jacket, I knew he was a veteran living on a 6000 ruble-a-month pension. 6000 rubles. Less than three dollars. He was offering a cherished family treasure in trade for a month's wage.

With hands shaking worse than the old vet's, I handed him a twenty dollar bill, accepted the packet of coins, and left before he could think about it. At the head of the lane, I looked back and answered his good-by wave. I felt like a thief.

Doors of Paradise

It is late October, yet tourists are still swarming over the treasures of ancient Florence. When we leave the Hotel San Giorgio for the short walk to the Baptistery, the sky is dark and heavy with impending rain. We hurry through the crowding streets, past early morning delivery vans, vendors firing up their chestnut roasting barrels, and hungry beggars staking out their appointed spots. The Cathedral of Santa Maria del Fiore, or the Duomo as it is known to everyone, looms between buildings as we get closer to the old octagonal Baptistery. The massive bronze baptistery doors facing the towering facade of the Duomo across the square draw people like a magnet. This is a short visit and we are trying to concentrate on exploring the pictorial realism that led to the explosion of Renaissance art in Northern Italy. Designed by Lorenzo Ghiberti in the 15th century, the doors represent a new interest in the importance of man and his place in the natural world.

"Are the panels on these east doors all Old Testament depictions?" asked my husband.

"Yes," I said. "The earlier panels on the north doors have the New Testament stories."

"Let's take a minute and look at them," he said, walking around the stone building.

"Let me get this film loaded," I said. "I need to finish photographing the panels in the Jacob and Esau story."

"Hurry up then. We're going to get wet," he said. "Hey. Here's the Good Samaritan story."

"Where?" I answered. "Oh, these won't be very helpful. They are too old. They don't show any sense of space or perspective and look how stiff and wooden the people are."

"But look at that nice donkey."

"Yeah. Very nice."

"Aah. The rain. Get inside, quick."

It is dark and very crowded in the small building. The dull, crumbling frescos on the walls and ceiling fail to hold anyone's attention for very long so we migrate to the open doorway to watch the rain sheet down. Elbow to elbow we fidget and stew and think about lunch and being somewhere dry, comfortable, uncrowded. Standing behind the mob of people, I notice a tall, black-haired woman slip into the doorway. Dumping her child on the stone floor, she proceeds to remove the folded newspapers that serve as her rain gear. She is dressed in a pale green sari that would have been beautiful had it not been so stained and crusted with dirt. Her feet are bare, but the palms of her hands are carefully hennaed and her eyes look strangely theatrical under their load of mascara. When some of the more observant of the crowd move away from her, she quickly snatches her child from the littered floor. With one fluid motion she opens her sari, pulls out a huge, flaccid breast, and jams the child's mouth over it. The child is totally unresponsive and his head lolls back over the woman's arm, his dilated pupils unseeing. She finally succeeds by raising her arm at an unnatural angle with the child's head clamped vice-like in the crook of her elbow.

Surprised, I look closer and realize this baby is three or four years old and his mother has stopped lactating months ago. Grappling with the heavy child, the dark woman approaches my husband alternately demanding and begging money. Shoving the child in his face and tugging on his jacket, the woman succeeds in producing a small circus for the bored crowd. Embarrassed by what is happening to my husband, I look away and discover another circus. A blur of motion behind the woman's flowing dress reveals a second child. A liquid-eyed boy of eight or nine is quietly detaching himself from his mother. Below the eye level of the crowd, he threads his way around behind them, his small hands groping and searching unwary pockets and bags.

This malodorous child is slipping his paw under the edge of my husband's jacket before I finally understand what is happening.

"Baksheesh. Sir, a little money, please. For the baby. Dollars. Baksheesh."

"Get back. Leave me alone. Get your filthy hands off my coat!"

"Baksheesh. A tip. A little money. For food."

"Let me through, please."

"Go away."

Suddenly the crowd shifts and I find myself next to the ragged boy. He is taller and older than I first estimated and the stench of old dirt and sweet incense is overwhelming. Without thought, I hit him with my open hand. The blow lands squarely on the side of his head and he goes tumbling across the slippery marble floor. Before anyone can react, my husband grabs my arm and we run out into the pouring rain. By the time we reach our hotel we are soaked; yet I wash my hands over and over. The scent of our unsuccessful assailant lingers in my mind.

After changing our clothes, we hang our wet jeans and socks over the bathroom door and return to the square for lunch. The passing storm has left the air clean and the sky brilliant blue. The hordes of tourists move leisurely through the square, smiling and nodding to one another. From our sidewalk table I see a flurry of activity on the Duomo steps. Two uniformed policemen are confronting the woman in the green sari. She is gesturing dramatically in a futile attempt to communicate her defense. The "old" infant sprawls on the curb wailing and rubbing the drug-induced sleep from his eyes. Harsh breathing and little pig-like squeals herald a third officer dragging the older child along by the arm. Deflated, the woman stands quietly, waiting while the three policemen discuss the situation.

"What will happen to them?" said my husband. "They look so miserable."

"Who cares. Just so they get them off the street," I said. "Miserable vermin."

"They are probably hungry."

"Ha! They're part of a gang. Probably some of the richest people in Florence."

The three officers decide to hustle the small family out of the square. With her wailing baby over her shoulder, the woman in the green sari strides away between the two older policemen. The young, fresh-faced officer is left to deal with the boy. With a wink and a friendly grin, he grasps the boy by the shoulder and steers him through the crowd behind the others. The boy pleads with his eyes and up turned hands, then stiffens and lets loose with a large glob of green spittle that lands square on the officer's shiny black shoe.

TRAM 18

It is September in Budapest. Feeble sunlight touches the broken sidewalks and crusted monuments of Gellert ter as two scholars from the nearby Technical University wait at the tram stop. The Hungarian is busy reading a translation of *Huckleberry Finn* while the American is paging through last week's *USA Today*.

"I hope Tram 18 is running today," said the American to himself as he looked anxiously up and down the track. "These post-commie schedules can be erratic."

"That gentleman appears confused," thought the Hungarian. "I should try to help him."

"Hmm...this fellow wants to be friendly," thought the American, adjusting his backpack and saying aloud, "Do you speak English?"

"Most certainly. I speak English very well, thank you," replied the Hungarian settling his Homburg more firmly.

"Can you tell me how these trams are guided?" inquired the American, "I don't see anyone throwing switches or operating a steering mechanism. Yet Tram 18 travels the track straight along the Danube to Moszkva ter and then Tram 48 comes on the same track, makes a right-hand turn, and crosses the river to the Pest side."

"Yes, yes," said the Hungarian.

"These Russian-made trams are a mystery to me." puzzled the American. He knelt on the dusty cobblestones trying to peer underneath Tram 53 as it jerked to a stop. "However do they get these things to go in the right direction?"

"Yes," said the Hungarian.

"So. Can you shed some light on this?" asked the American, brushing the dust from his blue jeans. "Or is this outside your field of expertise?"

"Yes," said the Hungarian. "Tram 18 will be here in ten minutes."

"H-o-w d-o t-h-e-y s-t-e-e-r t-h-e t-r-a-m-s." the American asked.

"Ten minutes, sir," said the Hungarian. "We have very good trams here."

"No, no. How do th..."

"Tram 18 will be here in ten minutes."

Not So Far Away

The Phoenix Glass

The clouds sat low the day the bird-carrying stranger stopped at the wide spot on Highway 12. The usually crisp air blew misty humid through the pines. The high country lay obscured by cloud, cloud that hugged the mountains surrounding the bare-board structure housing the Hi-Way Rock and Gem, cloud that dripped the evergreens dark with morning rain, cloud that grayed Tuesday afternoon into deep monotony.

Hunched over the steering wheel, the bird-man had hit the brake hard when he saw the peeling sign advertising the Hi-Way Rock and Gem. Maybe this run-down shop would have the crystal he wanted to complete his set. Earth, air, fire, and water, he believed each of the elements of the universe was represented by a crystal. He had the crystals for earth, air, and water, but the fire crystal still eluded him and it was the most crucial of the four. Most of July had been spent on this search. Sometimes he wondered if it was just an excuse for aimlessly pounding the back roads, an excuse for quitting a dirty, dead-end job at the tie plant, an excuse for leaving friends and family, but then the old fears would return to renew his determination to find the fire crystal.

He knew people close to him felt his phobia had grown out of control, but this restless searching gave him a measure of relief he couldn't find at home or on the job or with friends. A growing sense of coming doom and disaster lodged in his gut. With patience thin as paper he wheeled the muffler-shot van into the gravel parking lot. A little flame of anticipation kindled next to the pang of hunger that had lain in his stomach for the last fifty miles. He thought maybe he should have eaten when he gassed up the van, but it seemed a waste of time. At least the stop would give him a break from the road and with luck he'd find a pop machine, and the crystal. He flipped off the ignition and reached over the back of the seat to gather up his traveling companions.

He shuffled into the rock shop at ten past two, wearing birds. The pair of brilliant azure macaw perched on his shoulder brought a gasp from the woman clerking in the shop. When she could look past the birds, she noted the man's dirty blond hair caught in the frayed collar of his thrift shop double-knit and his khaki pants slopped over the tops of toes-out canvas shoes. His hands were dark, nearly maroon, with ground-in dirt or grease or God knows what. Was he a mechanic or a painter? An old scar mingled with raw new wounds marked his uneven jaw, but his eyes echoed the blue of the birds riding his shoulder. Beautiful eyes, she thought. They could almost make a woman forget the rough skin and hands, the ragged clothes, the shuffling gait, but not the birds. There was no way to overlook those birds.

"May I help you find something?" The woman leaned on the counter next to the cash register where she pretended to work on a ledger. She gave the floppy bow on her blouse a nervous twist and propped her chin in her hands to examine the birds. She watched them as closely as she dared without seeming to stare at the man, himself. The birds looked dusty and their beaks opened and closed ominously. She wondered if they were ill or mistreated. "We don't see many parrots up here," she said to the man. "You must be traveling."

"Not parrots. They're macaws." The greasy fellow sneered at the woman and looked at her just long enough to see her whippet-thin body and graying, blond hair. He averted his eyes and reached up to fondle one of the birds, trying to cover the shaking of his hands in the gesture. Just my luck to run into a talker, he thought, looks more like a librarian than a rock hound. Aloud, he asked, "Where is this place anyway? What do they call it?"

"Ethel. This is the town of Ethel, same as the gasoline." As the words left her mouth she realized they told her age. How long had it been since gas was a choice between regular and ethyl? She remembered her job and straightened up, smoothing her tweed skirt to be sure it covered her knees. She was surprised to find herself taller than the customer. Maybe he's a wrestler. He certainly has the build for it anyway. "Ethel. Ethel, Washington," she repeated. "It's unincorporated. No post office."

"What?" He found it hard to concentrate on the clerk's words. He never was much for conversation with strangers, especially women. He took one of the large birds on his stained finger and cradled the creature to his chest. The bird fit comfortably in the bend of his elbow. The warmth of the bird seeped through his shirt and gave him a sense of home, a feeling of connection, which lulled him into a moment of security. Then he realized the trickery of his senses and snapped at the woman, "What're you talking about, lady?"

"Ethel, like Lucy's neighbor on television. You have seen television, haven't you?" She tensed with surprise at her own sarcasm. She had long practiced the art of remaining impersonal with people, both here and at her regular job back home in Denver, and the slip worried her. Vaguely uneasy, she watched as the man rummaged through a rack of bolo ties with his free hand. "Everything's half-off. We're selling out," she told him. She continued with the pre-arranged speech she gave most customers, while she studied the man. "We still have most of the jewelry making supplies and quite a few finished pieces."

"Got any crystals?" His sudden move to peer into the rock bins along the wall startled the birds and they screamed shrilly. "Shut up Jolly, shut up Jersey." His voice was loud, almost a bark, cutting through the shrilling of the birds. He wanted to tell the scrawny woman to shut up, too, but decided it wasn't worth the hassle. "They do that when they get scared. Don't nobody scare my birds."

"Aren't they heavy?" She moved away, both fascinated and repulsed. She didn't like pets. You got attached to them and then they died. She hated the gold fish her parents had given her on her seventh birthday and had never begged for a puppy or a kitten like her friends. "Estate sale. We're having an estate sale. On account of my aunt and uncle were killed in a car crash and none of the kids want the rock shop." She realized she was babbling nervously, but unable to stop, she continued, "Just not interested in rocks and gems. All that cutting and polishing and making up the rings and jewelry and traveling to shows. You know. It takes a lot of passion to run a rock shop."

"Here, lady. You can hold Jolly." The man abruptly thrust the dusty bird onto her arm. "Don't move fast. His claws'll feel kinda hard, sharp-like, but you won't notice after awhile." Feathers swirled as the bird settled on the woman's bare arm, but she didn't flinch or cry out. "My name's Jackson," he said. The look of disgust and fear that crossed the woman's face fascinated him. The man almost smiled, tweaking his lip upward to showcase a gold tooth in his narrow face. Maybe this woman would be different from the others. Usually they screamed a demand he take the bird back or they would shake the bird from their arm. He smiled for real and asked, "What's your name?"

"Rose. Rose Barlow. Miss Barlow to you." The woman repressed the impulse to fling the bird from her arm. The hard, waxy feet of the bird and his sweet-sour odor forced her mind back, back to a time before the goldfish. She must have been five when she was sent to stay on the farm with her grandfather. He made her hold the chickens while he chopped off their heads. She was desperate to please her grandfather, but she also wanted to plead for the life of one special rooster. He was a runty black and white chicken who would follow her to the mailbox and leap into her arms when she came with the feed. It tore her heart when she held him by the feet for her grandfather to kill. With a sharp intake of breath Rose jerked back to the present and remembered the customer's query. She pointed to a chrome-legged table under the window. "I think there's some fluorite specimens over there. And some pink quartz and a kind of clear crystal. All the rock samples are half off, too."

"I'm into crystals, big time." Jackson reached inside his shirt and pulled out a plum-colored stone on a leather thong. The deep, translucent gem sent stabs of colored light over the gray walls of the rock shop. "This one keeps me strong. Protects me from evil spirits. Bad things in the air. Know what this here stone is called?"

"No. I don't know much about rocks." Rose felt dizzy watching the streaks of light rocket around the room. The mealy, almost rotten smell of the bird on her arm added to the unreal atmosphere in the old building. "It's real pretty, though." A wave of nausea welled up in the back of her throat and she struggled with the hysteria that threatened her. Take it easy, she told herself. He'll go in a few minutes. "We don't stock things like that." But she wished she did, so she could satisfy the man's demand.

"Anything interesting to see around here?" Kneeling, Jackson fingered through a bin of crystals on the floor, searching for the smooth, the clear, the flawless fit for his hand. He thought about the polished lump of serpentine he had bought the day before, smooth as silk and dark, dark green. The man had tried to tell him it was Columbia River jade, but Jackson knew better. Not that it mattered. He loved the way it fit round in his cupped palm. He barely noticed when the long-tailed bird clawed up his arm to the top of his head. "Damn you, Jersey. Get off me," he snarled at Jersey, but made no move to shift the bird to a more comfortable position. Need to ask her if there's a place to eat around here, too. "Well, is there? Anything to see around here?"

"I don't know much about this part of the country." And I don't want to know about it either. Rose suddenly realized how deeply she resented the family tragedy that had thrust her into this job of clearing up the affairs of the dead What did she care about this depressed bit of mountain with its population of out-of-work loggers and a few wildly enthusiastic intruders making trouble under the guise of protecting some invisible creature living in the forest. She consoled herself with the thought that it would soon be over and she could return to her apartment in Denver. Here with her brother, to dispose of the shop and the clap-board house in town, Rose found herself doing most of the work while her brother used the trip as an excuse for fishing the small streams running from the mountain glaciers. "It's a pretty boring place. Not even a movie theater or a decent restaurant."

"Must be something to see here." Jackson blew the dust off a piece of pink quartz and held it up to the light. "Junk," he muttered and tossed the rock back into the bin. Another wasted day, he thought. Why can't these people have the things he wanted? Who do they think will buy this crap, anyway? "I want a red tourmaline crystal; rubellite it's called."

Fascinated, almost mesmerized, by the bird perched on the man's head, Rose tried to remember if she had seen any rock specimens labeled rubellite. She almost demanded the stranger retrieve the bird perched on her arm so she could look for it. She disliked whining or complaining by others and most of all, by herself. "Is this rock valuable?"

"Crystal, a three-sided crystal. Deep red. It can focus a person's energy and clear their thoughts." And protect him from fire, which was something he particularly feared. Jackson picked up some polished agate, then slammed it back into the bin when he saw the flaws tracing across its under surface. "More junk. Why do people come to this part of the country? Is there natural stuff, like waterfalls or rock formations? Campgrounds? Some place to eat?"

"The biggest attraction is Mount St. Helens." Rose jumped as Jolly tightened his grip on her arm. Though she had never been there, herself, she heard about the newly formed volcano from almost every customer. "The volcano, you know?"

"Where's that?" Jackson stood up suddenly and turned to face the woman. He had forgotten about putting the other bird on her arm and jerked back in surprise. The woman looked pale and ethereal coupled with the vivid macaw. He had thought her dull and faded, a spinster librarian, maybe. But in this instant she radiated the aura of an alien goddess with silvery-gold hair spread fan-like from her sharp, translucent features. Then the light changed and the moment passed. The bird perched in his hair squalled and flapped to keep his balance, but the young man ignored the ruckus on his head. "Is it cold there? My birds don't like the cold."

"Which way are you traveling?" She glanced at the muddy van parked lonely in the shop's lot. Would that old clunker make it up the steep mountain road? She doubted it. "The highway is well marked."

"From California." He retrieved Jersey from his head and settled him on the glass counter top. The creature's black eyes looked like knobs of polished obsidian peering at its turquoise reflection in the glass. "I'm sorta on vacation." The thought of visiting a volcano both intrigued and frightened him. "Is it a real volcano, with fire and lava?"

"If you drove up from the south, you passed the turn off on your way here." She cautiously tried to dislodge Jolly from her arm, but his grip was firm. She wondered how anyone could not know about Mount St. Helens. And not see the large and numerous highway signs pointing to the road up the mountain. "Guess it's about as cold as mountains usually are. Mostly it's windy."

With great concentration, Rose shrugged Jolly from her arm to the counter without touching him with her hands. Like stepping on the cracks in the old children's game, she knew she couldn't touch the bird with her hands. She gave a little gasp of relief when Jolly thumped down beside Jersey. She rubbed the red marks on her arm and went to the shop window to pick up an iridescent glass globe from the display. Holding the purple-streaked ornament to the light for the stranger to see, she told him, "This is made from the ash that rained out of the volcano. Some people believe it has special powers."

"Ashes? How can you make anything out of ashes?." Glass that grew from the fire of a volcano might have the power of the red crystal. It might have the power to make him forget the flames of the great burning. Forget the year he had worked on a horse farm where an outbreak of anthrax necessitated the destruction of dozens of horses. Two-year olds in training, brood mares, stable ponies, even the foals, the babies. His job was to burn the carcasses in huge funeral pyres to prevent the spread of the deadly infection. Jackson rubbed his eyes as if to rub away that terrible vision, then walked past the drooping birds on the counter to join Rose by the window. "Let me feel it."

"Careful," she warned him. "It's fragile." His hot fingers touched hers when she passed him the glass ball. Rose gasped and jerked her hand away as if from a snake. Nearly dropping the ornament, she looked up to catch Jackson watching her. "I'm sorry," she stammered. "You surprised me." She remained standing at his elbow, close enough to breathe the musky smokiness of the man. In spite of his strangeness, or perhaps because of it, Rose knew she was drawn to him. And then again, maybe she'd just lived alone far too long.

Jackson palmed the globe; rubbed it with his thick, hang-nailed thumb, mumbling, "Phoenix glass. Up from the ashes. From death into life." Then he sniffed its swirled surface of blue and purple and duck's-neck green. Finally, he put the glass to his cracked lips and licked its ridged and valleyed surface. A wave of bliss murmured across his face and briefly wiped away the hard lines of discontent scoring it. "I need this, lady. How much?"

"More than you can afford." Alarmed at the stranger's intensity and her own feelings, Rose wondered if it was time for her brother to arrive at the shop to take his turn at the cash register. He was usually willing to watch the store a few hours while she went for groceries and cooked supper. Glancing around, she stole a look at the clock. It still read seven thirty. Damn, she thought. It's stopped again.

"We'll see." Jackson held the glass ball with tenderness while he turned to continue searching through the rock bins for a red crystal. Absorbed in his search, he crooned to himself. Flashing crystals and broad-winged birds whirlpooled with pale spirit women and aqua globes in his brain. Lost in his fantasy world, Jackson was unaware of the birds on the counter and heedless of the thin woman as she retreated towards the back of the shop. The birds preened and clacked their beaks together. A brief flare of sunlight revealed a cloud of dander and small feathers settling over them, setting them apart like figures in a snow dome. They seemed to sway in time to Jackson's droning song. "Hush little birdies don't say a peep papa's gonna get you a rose to keep   and if that rose don't sing   papa's gonna give that rose a fling." Was he thinking about hurting Rose? That's not nice, Jackson told himself. I'm done with that sort of thing. He stared into the green depths of the glass pool he held in his hand, then shook his head.

"I'll be back in a minute." Rose walked to the rear of the store and slipped into the restroom before she could hear the last lines of Jackson's song. Mostly, she wanted to wash the stink of the bird from her arm, but she also needed to collect her thoughts. She shot the bolt of the door behind her. How many coats of enamel crusted the old door, anyway? Rose ran her forefinger up the door frame and rained bits of seafoam green, peach, and iron gray chips onto the worn linoleum floor. She turned and leaned against the door. When she raised her eyes from the floor, she startled at the haggard woman facing her in the mirror. The crazed glass emphasized the dark circles under her eyes and deepened the creases along her mouth. The dim forty-watt over the sink cast a yellow pallor on her skin reminiscent of a long ago bout with some illness. Rose thought about the blue-eyed man while she applied fresh lipstick. Jackson's ramblings about the Phoenix rising from the ashes bothered her, but not as much as the man, himself. Get a grip, woman. He's just a rock hound. A not very clean guy out bumming round the country. The shrilling phone cut clear to the soles of her feet. She worked to open the sticky latch, but the ringing stopped abruptly before she could get the door open.

When she returned to the store front, Jackson was placing the phone in its cradle. "That was your brother," he reported. "Said to tell you he wouldn't be in today. Figured you wouldn't mind." His eyes, sharply bright next to the duller blue of the parrots on the counter, bore into her soul and traced the shudder which rippled down her body. "You don't, do you, Rose?"

"Did he want me to call back?" Rose hoped for a chance to hear a familiar voice. She needed an anchor in this odd, uncertain day. "Did he leave a number?"

"No. No number." Jackson grinned and played with the birds. He teased Jolly into grasping his finger with his beak, then lifted the bird from the counter. Not as fun as baiting this pinch-mouthed woman, though. "Said he was going fishing. Seems odd to be fishing in this weather." Jackson yo-yoed the bird up and down with his out-stretched hand. "You like fishing, Rose?"

"Did you find anything you wanted?" Rose watched the bird swinging from Jackson's out-stretched finger like a subject being entranced by a hypnotist. She hardly noticed the darkening room as her eyes followed the motion. A sheer quiver of fear brushed across her shoulders and was gone before she could name it. "The bird could fall," she whispered. "Don't hurt him." Rose felt responsible for all the bits of petty tragedy in her world. She often thought she preferred huge problems like war and famine to the small accidents of daily life because someone bigger and better would surely step forward to take care of important tragedies. Louder and more insistent she said, "Please be careful."

"It's hard to tell the males from the females." Jackson continued to wave the bird up and down, backward and forward. Ignoring the bird, he stared at Rose, confining her in his blue gaze. "I don't know if these are males, females, or one of each."

"That's interesting." Rose desperately wished the conversation onto a different track. But, feeling the need to soothe this man, she asked, "What do zoos and aviaries do about mating their birds, then?"

"You're blushing, Rose. A blushing, blooming rose, you are." He fondled the glass ball, cupping it to his shoulder. He continued to tease the macaw up and down on his finger, unaware of the bird in his pursuit of Rose's discomfort. Jackson knew he should take the birds and leave, but something about this lonely woman held him. He teased her in the same cruel, slightly dangerous way he teased the bird to insulate his feelings. "This'll be good for me," he told her. He held the green glass to the light and caressed it with his eyes.

"Nonsense. It's just a bauble, a gee-gaw, tourist junk." Rose slumped against the counter, tired of the game, jealous of a handful of blown glass. She wanted him, wanted to touch him, wanted to stroke him like she had wanted to pet a wild and dangerous tiger at an animal park once. How would it feel to be treated like a precious ornament? To be caressed and ogled and held tight against a sweaty chest by a blue-eyed stranger? Part of her longed for an easy chair, hot coffee, privacy, but it wasn't strong enough to overcome the vividness of the stranger's spell. "You want me to wrap it for you?" she asked, willing him to answer, yes, but no longer aware of what she offered him.

"You said it was special." Jackson scowled at the ornament and rubbed it against his pants as if to remove the tarnish of her words. Why did things always start out so bright and hopeful for him and then go so wrong, so dim and ugly? It seemed like everyone was against him. "What are you trying to pull, rock-lady?"

A sudden clash on the metal roof of the shop jumped Rose back to her senses. What was wrong with her, anyway? Maybe she had watched too many soap operas on the small TV in the back room of the shop these last weeks. She hurried to the door to investigate the noise and saw a branch leaning off the edge of the roof. The wind had wrenched it free from a half-dead maple tree. She paused to watch the rain from gathered storm clouds pelt down through the leaves. Storm clouds formed up in her mind, too. She fingered the car keys in her pocket and considered walking out into the rain and around the corner of the shop to her car. She could imagine herself sliding behind the wheel and driving down Highway 12 to the interstate where she would head south, away from the rock shop, away from the bird man, away from the trauma of her aunt and uncle's death, away from responsibility and reason. She could just walk out through the rain and start over where no one knew her. She could break free from her past like the branch breaking away from the old tree. She would become the Rose of her imagination, spontaneous, sexy, adventuresome. A roll of thunder and the bird man's voice pierced her pleasant vision.

"What're you doing over there, shop lady? You're supposed to be taking care of your customers." Jackson whirled suddenly and the bird lost his hold, crashing to the floor, hard. The macaw lay spread on the concrete, unmoving, but for a fitful twitching of his scaly legs. "See what you made me do, lady." Jackson's voice rose to shrillness as panic gripped him. "You did this." He scooped up the bird and held it close. The bird shivered and murmured, but his head hung limp across the man's arm.

"I'm so sorry." Why did she always feel so guilty when something went wrong? Why did she need to fix everything? Rose rushed back to the counter. "Is he dead? No. I can feel his breast moving." She felt only vaguely sorry for the injured bird, yet she felt a giant hand squeeze her chest and her heart seemed to jump with anxiety. It was like she had broken something ugly that meant a great deal to someone close to her. "There's a veterinarian over in Chehalis. We can take him there."

"No. No, I can't do that." Jackson shivered as hard as the bird, tears running down his battered face. His experience with animals on the farm led him to believe that the injured were quickly put out of their misery. Calves and colts and cows were shot, while smaller animals were dispatched with a blow from the back of a shovel. The veterinarian was called for difficult births, but usually so late that he could do little. Except for the anthrax thing when the vet showed up with two Department of Agriculture officials who declared outwardly healthy animals infected and said they had to be put down immediately. No, he couldn't go to a veterinarian with his bird. "No doctors. I'll take care of him."

"Your bird needs help." Rose was standing so close she could feel Jackson trembling. She raised her hand and traced the tattoo on his forearm. When he didn't react, she moved her hand to his shoulder. But, when she tried to examine the bird, Jackson elbowed her away. He kept a tight grip on both the bird and the translucent glass ball, unwilling to let go of either. "Please let me take him to the vet," she begged. Anything to put things right, she thought. "If it's money you're worried about, I'll pay for it."

Jackson abruptly changed his mind and shouted at Rose, "Hold him till I get back." When he thrust the bird into Rose's arms, he knew he could trust her to keep the bird from further harm for a few minutes. "Wait right there." Jackson slammed out the door and ran through the rain to his van. I've got to end this, he thought. I can't let him suffer and I can't trust some doctor. There's nothing else can I do.

As she struggled to hold the macaw without causing him any more pain, Rose could feel the movement of his broken wing bone. Her fear of touching the bird overcome, she looked around for a scarf or a rag she could use to bind the creature's wing and prevent further injury. In her mind the blue of the macaw merged with the black and white of the little rooster and her stomach lurched.

"I'll fix it," shouted Jackson. As he burst into the shop with rain-dark hair plastered to his skull and water running from his clothes, he knew what he had to do. He left the front door to bang in the rising wind as he puddled across the floor. He held a long barreled pistol in his right hand. The volcanic ash ball was clutched in his left. "Put the bird on the floor, over there." With the pistol, he gestured towards the bare cement wall at the back of the store, where a pile of boxes and old wooden crates awaited disposal. "Now."

"What are you going to do?" Knees turned to jelly, Rose could already see the bird a wasted, tattered rag of blue feathers, cold against the dirty floor of the shop, or bloodied from the chop of a sharp hatchet. "You can't kill him."

"Why not? He's my bird. I can do anything I want

with him." He shouldered her to the back of the shop, one outstretched hand holding the pistol, the other the glass globe. He was puzzled at her resistance, not understanding why she could passionately defend the injured bird. "Want to do something about it?" He had to shout to be heard over the wind, wind that blasted trails of paper and wet leaves through the open door, wind that slashed stacks of old gem magazines and store records from the counter and sent them slapping against the back wall of the shop where Rose and the bird cowered. "Want to do something about it?" he screamed again. "I can't let him suffer."

"You're crazy," said Rose. But as soon as the thought was voiced, she knew she didn't believe it. The only insanity in this room was her own. She knelt on the rough floor with the parrot across her thighs, oblivious to the sting of sweat in her eyes and the noisy gasping of her own breathing. She didn't notice her skirt hiked up to reveal the darker tops of her hose. She wasn't aware of her blouse half undone and her hair lank and heavy across her face. "It's only a broken wing. It will heal." She saw no change in Jackson's face and tried a different approach. "Think of the Phoenix. Your plum stone can help Jolly get well after the veterinarian sets his wing."

"Why are you so sure?" Jackson paused and looked at the woman while he thought about the power of the crystal. Maybe she had something there. Did he really believe in the lore of the crystal? For the first time he saw Rose as a real person, an ally. Maybe she offered a solution, but he needed assurance. "Doctors just make things worse. Sometimes they kill animals."

"This is your pet, your friend. If you shoot him, he'll be dead, too." Rose looked up at Jackson while her long fingers probed and kneaded the bird's rough feathers. The room spun. She felt detached from her body, held only by the thread of her contact with the bird through her finger tips. The cold damp of the floor worked through her skirt and her knees ached from the unnatural position. Still she pleaded, "Give him a chance."

"Can't let him suffer. Move, lady." Jackson stood above her, his legs spread to give him a firmer stance. "I've got to do this. Please."

"You can't," she screamed at him. "Please. Put the gun away."

"I can," he howled back, but his resolve had weakened. "I can and I will." A crescendo of thunder shook the building and the lights flickered. With a sharp intake of breathe Jackson knelt on the floor facing Rose and placed the pistol and the Phoenix glass between them. He touched her face with the back of his hand and found it wet with tears. "Don't cry, Rose." Then he pushed her hair back out her eyes and cupped her face between his palms. How strange, her face fits my hands like the green serpentine stone. Aloud he said, "Let me take the bird. I won't cause any more pain."

"Please go." Rose shifted the bird to the floor next to the pistol, but made no move to shake off the man's rough hands. "You can take the Phoenix glass and I'll take the bird. We'll trade. You can even stop by here in a couple of weeks and pick up the bird when he's well."

"Why would you do that? Take so much trouble and all?" Jackson tried to soothe Rose like he would quiet a nervous horse. He brushed her hair back, buttoned her blouse, and straightened her collar. Still kneeling in front of her, Jackson took hold of her hands and raised them to his cheek. "You don't even like the bird."

"It would be such a waste." Neither Rose, nor Jackson knew if she referred to the bird or to Jackson, himself. A calm silence filtered through the building as the wind died down and the pounding rain turned to drizzle. Rose knew the danger was past, but needed to confirm it. "Come on, Jackson. You don't want to shoot anything. It'll cause no end of trouble."

"I'll stop back the end of July." Jackson let go of her hands, then stood up and stuck the pistol in his belt. "Will that be soon enough?"

"Take the volcano glass. Maybe it'll be your lucky piece." Still on her knees she held the shining ball up to him. Just then the sun broke through the clouds. The light caught the glass and sent green and blue triangles wheeling around the room.

~~~~~

This story grew from a trip to Washington State a few years after the eruption of Mount St. Helens. With time on our hands while waiting to see a local businessman we drove the back roads 'just looking.' We stopped at several rock shops including one with a 'going out of business' banner above the door. The clerk and her story is pretty much verbatim. The fellow with the birds came in as we were leaving, so his back story was all invented.

~~~~~

Walk To The Sun

Long ago Snoqualm, the Moon, ruled the heavens. One day he asked Spider to make a rope of cedar bark and stretch it from the earth to the sky. Beaver, one of the animals living on the earth, discovered the rope and climbed up to the sky. Once there, Beaver waited until the Moon was asleep, then he began exploring the Moon House and the Sky World. He found a forest of fir and pine and cedar trees. He pulled some of them up by their roots and then, with his spirit powers, made them small enough to carry under one arm. Under his other arm, he put the tools for making daylight. He gathered up some fire from below the smoke hole of the Moon House and wrapped it in ashes and leaves so he could carry it safely. He found the sun hidden beneath some blankets and stole it too. Down the rope went Beaver, back to his home on earth, where he planted the trees and made daylight. He set the sun in its place to give heat and light to all. Everyone was very happy because of the things Beaver brought from the sky.

About this time the Moon awoke and discovered the sun was missing from its hiding place. Angry and suspicious, he knew that one of the earth people had tricked him. Seeing footprints outside the Moon House, he followed them to the top of the rope which Spider had made. "I will follow the culprit to Earth and get my sun back." But as he started down the rope which Spider had made, it broke. Both Moon and rope fell down in a heap. They were transformed into a mountain, known as Mount Moon or Mount Snoqualmie in the Suquamish language to this very day. [From a Suquamish Indian Myth]

And to this very day the inhabitants of earth play in the forest under the watching sun and some of them run afoul of anger and suspicion and fall down in a heap like Moon. Fourth of July weekend many people and a few dogs went out to play in the forest under the sun on Mount Snoqualmie. Not all of them came back to play another day.

This July day opened hot and dead still on Snoqualmie Pass, the low crossing of the north Cascades. The rocky peaks at the summit rose like steel blades from the surrounding hills. Lines of dark fir trees ran jagged up the mountain's crest to touch the sun.

"You about ready?" Gail burst into the dorm room, all sweat and muscle and hundred watt energy. "Everything's in the car except Ripper."

"I appreciate you taking me along." Methodically, Lesley gathered up film and filters and arranged them in the battered camera bag along with the camera she had checked out from the photography department. "I need this assignment."

"Said I would, didn't I?" Gail looked uncomfortable. "You saved my neck writing that English comp paper."

"Hope I get some decent photos." Lesley slung the case over her shoulder. "Back to nature. Where do they get off telling us to photograph trees as a metaphor of the human condition?"

"Four day weekend, here we come." Gail shoved Lesley into the hallway and slammed the door behind them. "Ripper's tied to the bike rack downstairs."

"I don't know why we need to take that dog along?" Lesley stopped at the vending machine in the lounge and fed it a handful of quarters. She stowed the assortment in her camera case. "Never know when you'll need a little quick energy."

"Excuses. Excuses. Admit it, Lesley, you just like to eat."

The girls' destination was Snoqualmie Pass where the old Sunset Highway cuts across the mountains. This is the lowest crossing of the north Cascade Mountains in Washington State, but it is still high enough to keep the summers cool. This July day was the exception to the rule and the half-dozen cars parked in the visitor's lot at the pass radiated heat. The throbbing sun beat down on the usually mist shrouded mountain. The rocky peaks at the summit rose like steel blades from the surrounding hills and lines of dark fir slumped up the craggy granite to touch the sky. The mountain shimmered in the glare, threatening to topple onto the hapless ant people in the parking area below.

Gail, Lesley, and Ripper arrived at the trail head parking lot after a two hour drive fighting holiday traffic for Gail. Two hours of sneezing and itchy, red-eyes for Lesley. Cooped in Gail's small car with a dog was Lesley's vision of Hell, itself. The young women and the dog piled out of the car with sighs and whimpers of relief. A wheezing Lesley and a sympathetic Gail unloaded camping gear from the blue compact and piled it on the asphalt as they prepared to hike the section of Pacific Crest Trail which snakes down the crest of the mountain range to Gravel Lake. Short and easy or so they thought. They sorted and organized their equipment, while Ripper investigated the tires of the car in the next parking slot.

A different kind of camper put the finishing touches on his camping outfit in a small clearing under the interstate bridge on the other side of the summit. He walked out to the dirt road he had driven in on to see if his vehicle was visible to passing motorists. Satisfied that the brown truck faded to invisibility through the trees from the distance of the road, he returned to pick up his backpack and the open bottle of whiskey next to it. He took a pull from the bottle and swished it around in his mouth. Damn tooth ache, he muttered to the wind.

His muddy boots crushed the ferns and delicate wildflowers as he searched for the old forest service track. He tried to place long crumbled landmarks from boyhood memories in the surreal setting of the huge concrete pillars of the interstate. The highway towered so far above his head that he could hear only the loudest of the eighteen wheelers as they down-shifted on the crest grade of Snoqualmie. He remembered the thrill and disgust and anger he felt when he watched the prefab sections of the bridge being lowered into place by helicopter. The government was so careful not to damage the environment, the precious ecosystem of the old growth forest, when they constructed that last segment of interstate. So careful and protective of trees and ferns and little animals, but they destroyed my father's life, Alfred thought. The government's highway and that old hag, Ruby. Forgetting where he was for an instant, he slammed the half-empty whiskey bottle against the concrete bridge pillar. I'll show them they can't push Alfred Blainey Jr. around.

Gail finished packing up the few odds and ends she had tossed into the car after a last minute stop at the mini-mart. She usually stowed the basics in her pack before leaving the dorm, but absently forgot the trail map and her tooth brush this time. She had other things on her mind, like her upcoming senior year at the university. Two more semesters and she would be free to get on with real life. She wondered how her new boy friend, Robbie, was amusing himself this weekend. Good natured Robbie had loaned them Ripper for the camping trip after he found he had a last minute appointment. Maybe he could join them at the lake. Gail examined her face in the side mirror of the car, wrinkled her nose at the image staring back at her. Not bad, maybe even attractive; or at least healthy and well-conditioned in a race horse sort of way. Glowing, maybe that's a good description. She felt like prancing and parading this morning. Too bad there isn't much of an audience. Maybe I should change my major to theater, she thought.

Lesley watched Gail examine her image in the car mirror, then, with a stab of envy, turned away. Lesley admired her roommate, but that didn't keep her from envying Gail's slender figure and long dark hair.

"Want to go to the movies with Robbie and me when we get back?" Gail thought Lesley looked a bit peaked. Maybe it was just the light. "Robbie has a friend he could fix you up with. He's in forestry or botany or something like that."

"No thanks." Lesley popped her gum a few times, then fished around in her pocket for the wrapper so she could dispose of it. "I've got a paper to finish and I'll have to develop the film I shoot this weekend. What I really need is an aspirin."

He kicked at the fragments of the shattered

whiskey bottle and sucked his throbbing molar. For a moment, Alfred wondered if this was a bad omen. No, that was busted mirrors and anyway, he had another fifth in his pack. He stomped back to the forest edge to resume his hunt for the old track that wound up the mountain to Gravel Lake. Two unsuccessful passes through the area that should have revealed a gap in the granite ridge, left Alfred fuming with anger. On the third try he stepped into a brush covered hole and nearly twisted his ankle. He threw down his pack and tried to reason his way out of the impasse. Must be a way to find the path.

think, man, think   this is important   don't let those murdering government boys pull one over on you there's a landmark here somewhere   somewhere harder   look harder   slow down

His forehead wrinkled with concentration as he slowly scanned the clearing in the forest. Most of the vegetation seemed untouched by man or beast. Had we really lived here?

maybe I can find the remains of the old house   the foundation was rock and concrete   should be some trace   aagh the bulldozer   crunching doors   window frames   spitting up pink insulation
yellow front end loader scooping up the mess
 hauling it out of the clearing   I miss that house   so safe warm

 we never   never   let Ruby in that house   did we

Daddy   nobody ever hurt me there   I miss you Daddy
that threshold stone should be here   hand-hewn that
stone was   under the front door   might still be here
somewhere somewhere

Alfred finally spotted a slight unevenness in the
long grass of the clearing. He knelt on the spongy pelt of
grass and prodded the dirt with one splayed, broken-
nailed forefinger, then pulled a long-bladed gutting knife
from the sheath on his belt. With the knife he carefully
probed the mound until it struck a hard core a few
inches beneath the soil. With a sturdy stick Alfred quickly
uncovered the oblong stone and determined the rough
outline of square foundation blocks running parallel to
the big marker stone. Now, he thought, I can find the
track because it ran straight away from the back of the
house. He wiped the blade on his pant leg and returned
it to its sheath. He shouldered his pack with a grunt and
scrambled through a thick stand of fern to disappear
down the faint track into the forest.

"Do you need help?" Gail propped her gear against
the car and knelt beside Lesley who sat on the curb,
nodding and bouncing in time to the silent rhythms
pouring from the walkman clipped to her belt. "With
your gear, I mean, not the great American novel or the
last word in photo journalism or whatever it is you're
thinking about."

"I wish." Lesley closed the notebook she had

balanced on her knee, then stuck the chewed yellow pencil in her hair. "University is harder than I thought it would be. Maybe I should've stayed at the community college."

"You don't mean that. The first year is always the worst." Gail shucked off her pullover and fingered the sleeve of the flannel shirt Lesley wore. "It's going to get hot. Did you bring a cooler shirt? This thing looks like a pajama top."

"I probably have something here somewhere." Lesley dumped her pack out on the black top and retrieved a chocolate bar from the heap. "Seems like a long time since breakfast."

"Do you get your clothes out of a church mission barrel?" Gail gingerly sorted through the mess. "Tie-dye peasant blouse, polyester slacks, square dance skirt with sequins. Good gravy, Lesley."

Lesley jammed a silk harem blouse into her pack. "I had to do my laundry, but the machine was broke, and then I couldn't find any change for the pay washer."

"A silk blouse? We're not going to a tea party."

"Sorry, Gail." Lesley grappled with a snarl of nylon rope, but gave up and threw it into her pack. "All my tee shirts were in the dirty clothes."

"You're hopeless." Gail began repacking Lesley's pack. "Bubblegum, chocolate-covered cherries, nylons. Didn't you read the list of things to pack?" Gail snorted and continued sorting. "Where's your waterproof match pack? And your bug repellent?"

"Do you think we'll find some neat old trees?" Lesley ignored the complaints. She was adept at tuning out, having had a lot of practice with three brothers at home. "I need to get some really great photos."

"There are trees behind the library." Gail finished arranging Lesley's belongings and leaned the pack against the car. She pulled her long hair back and secured it with a tie. "I'd just shoot a roll over there and be done with it. A tree's a tree."

He leaned against an enormous cedar to catch his breath, and slow his racing thoughts. Focus, Alfred, focus, slow down. He tried to shut out the red dagger of pain in his jaw by thinking about Ruby.   Ruby   Ruby   old hag   took advantage of his daddy   Ruby, the woman who hated him   bitchy Ruby who insisted his   daddy draw   out their savings   buy a new mobile home scar the mountain clearing with her improvements   old witch Ruby   signed   the   papers   when   the government boys wanted their land for the interstate sneaky conniving Ruby   signed his daddy into   the nursing home

      ugly old hag Ruby

Alfred pressed hard against the rough bark of the tree, a tree that was old when Captain Gray sailed up the Washington coast. He pulled the knife from his belt sheath and plunged it into the bark of the tree again and again, rasping the skin from his knuckles, but not knowing, not caring.

After the two girls had their own gear ready to go, they set about outfitting Ripper. The big dog wiggled and squirmed when Gail fastened the saddle bag to his blaze orange harness. He voiced a low throaty growl when she filled the pockets with packets of dry dog food and added a length of cable with snaps at either end.

"Maybe we ought to put his muzzle on now, Gail. He has to wear it on the trail anyway." The dog yelped and growled. Lesley jumped back. "Are you sure he's been trained to carry things?"

"What's to learn? Robbie said he was trained." Gail tightened the strap under the dog's chest and adjusted the nylon muzzle around his heavy jowls. Ripper rubbed against Gail's knee. "He likes me. He'll do whatever I want."

"We'd be safer without the dog," muttered Lesley. Aloud she said, "He's just scratching. Dogs don't change loyalties that easy."   Lesley laced up her new boots and took a few steps. "Do I have to wear these clunky things?"

"I told you to break them in, wear them around campus a week or so." Gail stuffed a rawhide chew in the dog's pack, then snapped the leash on his collar. The dog tried to bite at the bulky pockets hanging over his back, but the muzzle prevented it.

"So ugly. I couldn't wear them anywhere. Are we about ready?"

"I think so." Gail wrapped the leash around her hand. "Lock the car and we'll be off."

When the trail steepened, the big man had to hunch forward to keep his balance against the weight of the pack. A branch smacked him across the jaw and he let out an involuntary howl of pain. At the first level place in the trail he stopped and placed the heavy pack on the ground, careful not to jar it. He wrenched a bottle of pain killers from his shirt pocket and swallowed three. From the pack he fumbled a bottle of whiskey and gagged a couple of mouthfuls to wash down the pills. Sweat beaded his upper lip when he started to climb again.

the granite face should be just ahead   seems farther than I remembered   Gravel Lake must be close I'm at the tree line   don't remember all this loose rock hurry hurry

Lesley took a last look around, locked the car, and shouldered her pack. She realized she could have completed her photography assignment right here next to the parking lot. Trees of every shape and size in easy proximity. With a sigh she followed Gail and the dog across the parking lot to the forest edge, where half-a-dozen trails fanned out beneath the fir trees. Directional signs pointed the way to various trails and campgrounds.

"Do we want to go to Windy Pass?" Gail peered at the dim copy of a map she dug out of her pocket, the one she had extracted from the mini-mart clerk. "Doesn't sound right."

"Gravel Lake." Lesley muttered, trying to read the Forest Service bulletin tacked to a nearby tree. "That's where the first campground is supposed to be."

"Let me ask somebody. Just to be sure." Gail stopped a man coming out of the forest. "Is this the south trail? The trail to the closest campground."

"That's right. Trail appears to go east, but it turns south in a few minutes." The man expressed interest in the big dog. "You use him to help carry your stuff? I saw a couple with a llama for packing a few days ago. Prohibiting horses on the trails has inspired some interesting alternatives."

"He's for protection. Ripper just carries his own gear. Food, tie-out cable, chew toy, you know." Gail patted the dog who was intent on investigating the man's shoes. "He belongs to my boy friend."

"There's been several assaults and one murder, possibly two, out on the Crest Trail. All young women." The man watched the girls' faces to see their reaction. "You sure you should be out here alone?"

"Lots of other campers out this weekend." Gail didn't blink, but she felt queasy remembering the news accounts of the attacks. "Anyway, Ripper's pretty scary."

"If you say so. It has been a while since there's been trouble." The man stepped off the trail to let the trio pass. "Be extra careful crossing the granite face. They did some more blasting and it could be slippery."

"Let's go." Gail tugged Ripper's leash and headed down the trail into the forest. Her bare legs flashed in the sunlight peppering the darkness of the forest canopy. She looked totally at home there, like an exotic, sleek haired animal. Lesley looked more like a tourist with her flowered shirt, camera bouncing on her ample chest, and plump legs made paler by the contrast of her purple shorts.

Alfred continued up the steep trail, relieved that the pain pills had kicked in. Sweat sheened his forehead and dribbled down the back of his neck. The big vein in his temple pulsed in rhythm with his quickened breathing and echoed the dulled beating of his tooth. He shed his jacket and tossed it. Sweat soon peppered through his blue work shirt and trickled down the back of his jeans.

hurry, hurry   day half gone   need to set up camp people will be there   find a nice, secret spot   we'll show them   stupid campers   government murderers   old hag   Ruby   they'll be sorry

Shards of newly broken rock along the path caused Alfred to stop. He looked over the edge and was surprised to see a trail blasted across the granite far below him. We'll show them some real blasting come Fourth of July, Alfred said to himself.

"You didn't tell me people get murdered out here." Lesley rubbed her temples with her thumbs trying to subdue the ache that was creeping back. "Did you know?"

"It's been in the paper for weeks. Some nut set a fire at a nursing home and left notes threatening to shut down the whole forest system. He thinks it belongs to him and he wants it back."

"Maybe we should've stayed home." Lesley comforted herself with another candy bar.

"Things like that only happen to other people." Gail pulled the dog closer. "They get careless or maybe they're not very smart."

"Did Robbie say he might meet us at the campground?" But she found she was talking to the wind, so Lesley gave it up and trundled after Gail and Ripper. She soon forgot her headache and her worries in the overpowering beauty of the forest. Huge ferns, four foot devil's club, and carpets of white trillium under hundred year old red cedar gave the place an other-worldly quality. She breathed deeply, sure that the mountain air would make her feel better. Only the long, spiky thorns on the devil's club gave her pause. Those enormous, velvety leaves had an under surface of ugly danger.

Seeing the dog in his blaze-orange disappear around the turn of the path brought Lesley back to the task ahead of her. Her feet were beginning to hurt and she was hungry again.

By mid-afternoon the trio had reached the granite face of the mountain. Here the trail changed from shaded mossy path to sun bleached rock, complete with warning signs telling hikers to use extreme caution.

Reading the signs and trying to catch her breath, Lesley let her pack drop. Wiggling her aching shoulders, she sat down on a flat boulder. She watched Gail pour water into Ripper's dish. "Can I have a drink, too? It's been a long morning."

"Didn't you fill your water bottle before we left?" Gail looked at Lesley with a mixture of alarm and concern. "Are you feeling all right?"

"I guess so. I didn't think it would take so long to get to camp." Lesley unlaced her boots and rubbed her feet. "How much farther is it?"

"We just need to get across the rock. Gravel Creek isn't far." Gail handed her water bottle to Lesley. She pulled up her socks and tightened her shoe laces. "We need to be careful on this next part." She had a brief tussle with the dog, then managed to retrieve his dish and stick it back into his pack. "Time to go."

"Let me get my boots on." Lesley struggled with the stiff high tops. "They seem to get smaller every time I put them on."

"You're not getting blisters, are you?" Gail held the dog away from Lesley while she finished tying the leather laces. "What's wrong with you, Ripper?"

"His feet probably hurt." Lesley stood up, not letting Gail see how painful it was. "Back off, Ripper. Maybe Gail will carry us for awhile."

Gail led the way out onto the rock, with the dog next and Lesley bringing up the rear. The trail, newly blasted through the granite, was level, but narrow, with a steep drop on one side. Far below the sun glinted off the water of a mountain stream.

On the cliff above the girls Alfred was in a quandary trying to decide whether to continue along the dim and almost impassably steep track or try to pick his way down to the well defined trail below. The curve of the mountain obscured his view of the girls else he might have continued on the upper track.

One for the road murmured Alfred tipping the bottle and taking a drink   another pill too   don't need that tooth jabbing me at a bad spot on the way down might end me up in the drink   He giggled at his joke and placed the bottle of whiskey back in its nest among the dynamite, caps, and cord in his pack. Down on his knees he probed over the edge with one booted foot, while resting his weight on his forearms. He found a foothold and gingerly shifted his weight to test it. He worked to keep a firm grip on the ridge of rock, while finding another foothold. Soon he was completely over the edge with no turning back. He searched for a lower outcropping with his right foot and ducked his head as a red wasp shot past.

"Slow down a little," Lesley called. Gail was nearly out of sight around a bend in the trail, pulling the reluctant dog behind her. "Gail, wait up."

"Sorry. Guess I got anxious about getting across the rock." Ripper tried to turn around on the narrow trail and sent a shower of loose rock spewing off into the gorge. "Take it easy, boy, or we'll be hauling you out of that gully."

"Some gully." Lesley, glad to stop, breathed heavily. "You could hide an ocean liner down there."

"You hear something?"

"Just my wheezing and Ripper's panting."

"You two are definitely out of shape." Gail held her own breath so she could listen. "I'm sure I can hear something. Maybe up above us."

"How could there be anything up there except mountain goats?"

Alfred continued his hunt for a lower foothold, aware that his grip was not as secure as before. Sweat ran down his forehead into his eyes. His back muscles were beginning to cramp with the weight of the pack. The adrenal push he had received from earlier anger was beginning to wane, leaving a spreading weakness behind. He groped for a firmer hold, a branch, a rock, something he could fasten on so he could work the cramp from his back. Thoughts of whiskey flashed in his burning brain when he rattled his tooth awake. He shook sweaty hair from his face. Small rocks bounced down the slope when he kicked out trying to gain a safer foothold. Another red wasp joined the first one.

"Hush up, Ripper." Gail knelt beside the dog. "It's probably squirrels."

"You didn't put his muzzle back on after you watered him." Lesley watched the snarling dog warily. "He's really got his hackles up."

"Something's got his attention." Gail stood facing the slope. She shaded her eyes with her hand trying to see the ridge above. "I'll take his leash off and see what he does."

"Please, don't." Lesley cringed back against a boulder at the trail edge. "I don't trust him."

Forgetting his perilous hold on the rock, Alfred slapped at the wasp. His heavy pack slipped a fraction of an inch and with it, his center of gravity. His fingernails shrieked along the smooth rock where he grappled for a new hold. His feet scuffed and kicked at the cliff, feeling for solid ground. His mouth screwed up like a gill hooked carp, but no sound emerged. The red wasp lodged in the sweaty crease of his neck and sunk its stinger into the tender flesh below Alfred's ear. Rocks bounced past the frantic man to the trail below. The scream in his brain finally worked its way to the surface and erupted from his mouth.

"Check it out, Ripper." Gail stood up, coiled leash in hand, and watched the dog leap against the rocky outcrop. "That was a scream. Listen."

"Lot of rocks coming down." Lesley forgot about the dog. "I hear it, too. Somebody's up on the cliff."

"Sounds like pain." Gail stepped closer to Lesley. "Look out. That rock was a big one."

The girls edged back down the trail a short distance to an overhanging ledge that protected them from the falling rocks. Together they watched the man slide down the slope to the narrow path. A shower of rock and dirt came with him. He landed twisted on his side with one arm pinned to the ground under his chest. His momentum nearly pulled him from the trail. One leg hung out over empty air and his heavy pack threatened to tip him into the chasm. A thin line of blood welled out of the corner of his mouth and a large purple welt ballooned his throat beneath his ear. Before the girls could react, the black dog sprang forward.

Ripper dug his teeth into the kaki material of Alfred's backpack. His legs braced, the dog pulled the pack up over the man's head. The dog worried the rough material until he discovered it was not the man he was attacking. With a great shake of his jowls Ripper let go of the canvas and turned his attention to the man sprawled on the rocks. He snarled and showed his teeth under tight black gums, then he tore through the blue shirt and gripped Alfred's shoulder with granite hard teeth. This new stab of pain brought Alfred back to the edge of consciousness with a jolt. He could hear high-pitched voices screaming at the dog to back off. When the dog didn't loosen his hold, Alfred knew the animal was beyond control. He tried to lie very still and control his convulsive breathing. The dog's own breath was hot on his cheek.

"Gail, do something." Lesley dropped her pack and edged closer to the man on the path. "Ripper's going to kill him."

"Get back, Lesley." Gail slipped out of her pack and grabbed her friend's arm. "We don't know this guy. What's he doing up here, anyway?"

"He's hurt." Lesley forgot her headache and her sore feet. She forgot her fear of the dog. The bleeding man lay in danger of being pulled over the edge by his own backpack. "Help me drag his pack out of the way."

"Don't." Gail stepped back and let go of Lesley. "We need to find a ranger."

"No time." Lesley was careful not to pull in the direction of the chasm and risk sending the man rolling over the edge. She twitched the canvas bundle from his head and shoulders without touching him. One shoulder strap was ripped loose. He must have hung up on something. Lucky fellow. It probably broke his fall. Wary of the dog, she backed up, dragging the heavy load in stages until it lay in front of Gail. "This thing weighs a ton. Must be full of steel bars."

keep very, very still, Alfred muttered to himself play dead   can't let a scruffy dog spoil things the look on that pup's face when I rip him   split him end to end   don't kill him   make him suffer   payback time   pay back to you too Ruby

Deliberately, Alfred bit down on his bad tooth and was rewarded with enough pain to make him forget the dog with his teeth clamped into his shoulder. As the new pain overtook him, Alfred made a mental assessment of his body. Tensing thigh and calf muscles and wiggling his toes assured him that he hadn't broken legs or back in the fall. He turned his attention to the arm bent under him out of sight. He concentrated on flexing his fingers, one at a time, until he was sure he could grip with that hand. Slowly, slowly, he straightened his elbow under his chest out of sight.

the knife on my belt   can I reach the knife   did I lose it

"Lesley. Get back here." Gail had squashed her need to flee and had opened the man's backpack. "This thing is full of explosives. Dynamite."

"Maybe he's a park worker," Lesley called back.

She tried to remember the rudiments of first aid she had learned at swim camp the summer before. "He's bleeding from the mouth, but he does seem to be breathing."

"Maybe." Gail inched her way back up the trail." Her fear, coupled with the speed of the incident, left her shaky and light headed. "Maybe he has an I.D."

"If he has one, he's laying on it." Lesley couldn't decide if the man was breathing right or not. He seemed to be wheezing much like someone having an attack of some kind. She decided the bleeding was minor. But the dog, she had to make Gail get the dog away. "Try and make Ripper listen to you."

Gail vacillated between concern and panic, hardly able to think at all. Nausea plucked at the back of her throat. Her voice shrill, she tried to direct the dog. "Ripper, get back. Get back."

"You've got the leash in your hand." Lesley now saw that Gail was losing control. "Are you sure that's the right command?"

"I want to get out of here." Gail studied the blue nylon leash in her hand as if she had never seen such a thing before. A sudden groan from the man on the trail echoed through her brain. She tried to move forward, but her feet refused to obey. Lesley grabbed the leash and bent down to grasp the chrome ring on Ripper's harness. She held the ring between her thumb and index finger while she snapped the leash on it. Her hair sprawled loose from its tie and fell across her face. Through the strands of hair she looked at the man's face for the first time and found him staring at her. His eyes were pale gray with bloodshot whites. Lesley felt suddenly cold; blasted, chilled, by those eyes.

Through the haze of whiskey and pain killers and shock, Alfred saw the woman lean down towards him. His mind whirled back to the house in the clearing, the house forever gone. "Ruby," he croaked. "Ruby, you bitch. I'll kill you now. You won't get away this time." His gnarly hand shot out and grabbed Lesley's leg just above her hiking boot. His other hand, the hand pinned under his body, closed around the ridged leather handle of the gutting knife. With strength renewed by the surge of adrenaline pumped through his brain and body by his hatred of Ruby, Alfred pulled his knees up under his body and struggled to get up.

The dog refused to relinquish his hold. Gail screamed. Alfred slashed out at the tangle of hair, but the dog's weight on his shoulder ruined his aim. The knife missed Lesley and snagged her shirt. He tried to drag the screaming girl closer. His pull on her ankle nearly dropped her to the ground. She kicked at him, trying to free herself.

forget her for now   go for the dog   get rid of the devil dog   don't let go of her   he remembered   she'll run away   run   and tell   there will be hell to pay hell to pay   hell to pay   pay   pay

Gail picked her way up the trail towards where the dog snarled and worried the raving man. A bad dream, she thought. We're sleepwalking. Look at Lesley. I'll never get to her. The harsh glare of the sun on the white rock made the scene shimmer and shake with a terrible light. Look at her on the path so close to the dog, to the prone man. So intent that she missed seeing the man push himself up and slash out at Lesley again. By the time the scream penetrated her mind Lesley was on the ground kicking furiously at the man kneeling above her.

Bending down Gail found a sharp piece of granite. Rubble from the blasting, the rock was a perfect size to grip. A perfect weight for striking and crushing. For breaking, for hurting, thought Gail. An unexpected twist of excitement tore her chest and her heart raced. With her weapon she eased up the slope.

Lesley fainted back onto the rock and Alfred released his hold. He rubbed his hand across his eyes trying to clear his vision. He shook his head.

must be how the bull feels   tormented by the picador   harder   and harder to breathe   the wasp   where is it

He reached his hand to the swelling on his neck. The red wasp still clung there and he smashed it away in disgust. His fingers felt thick and slow. His tongue seemed too big for his mouth and a smoldering thirst griped him. With hands that obeyed only with extreme effort he began the slashing at the dog.

Methodically he worked the long-bladed knife into position. Because of the dog's grip on his shoulder, he buried his fingers in the it's pelt down below the rib cage. Right above the animal's soft belly. His free hand gripped the knife hard. Hard enough to whiten his bruised and bleeding knuckles. Trying to gain more leverage, he staggered to his feet. Dizziness and sharp howling licks of pain flicked at his consciousness like tongues of wind-blown flame. The dog refused to give up his hold even though he now hung off the man's body like a manic appendage.

Not knowing if Lesley was alive or dead, Gail stepped over her still form and tried to find an opportunity to use her primitive weapon. For a long, long minute of time the world stood still, quiet. The pageant of some strange melodrama unfolded on the mountain. Then she arced the sharp granite through the air with all her strength.

Alfred never saw the stone. The poison from the red wasp had triggered a reaction that caused a massive shut down of his system. Black fog blotted his vision as he labored to breathe. His mottled face tinged with blue. His knees buckled. The gutting knife dropped from his cold fingers. The dog released his grip, knowing, as animals do, that the man had become clay. Alfred Blainey Jr. sprawled dead on the ground. Gail's rock clattered over the edge and spun out of sight.

What have I done, thought Gail. Too weak to stand,

she collapsed on the trail. Hot tears washed her eyes. She wrapped her arms around herself, to still her trembling and to ward off the chill that swept her despite the hot summer sun. She wondered insanely if she were the only person left on earth. A sharp bark shattered her hysteria. Ripper was whimpering and licking her leg. Gail threw her arms around the big dog and hugged him close. He responded with full body wiggling and squirming. She ran her hands over the dog's body and found no gaping wounds, only a large bruise on his stomach where the man had grabbed him.

Gripping the dog's fur to steady herself, she crawled over to where Lesley lay. She talked to the dog, " Good dog, brave dog. What a mess. I killed him. Lesley, Lesley, please be all right." Gail held her breath when she turned her friend over. Lesley moaned and opened her eyes.

"What happened?" Dazed, but unhurt Lesley sat up and looked around. "What's wrong?"

"Are you all right?" With her arm around the dog's neck Gail tried to inspect Lesley for wounds and bruises. "I was really scared. I thought you might be dead."

Lesley suddenly remembered the man, the knife. "Where is he?" A surge of panic overcame her and she tried to get up.

Gail pushed her down. "He's dead. He can't hurt us." She spoke in a high whisper and wondered who she thought could hear. "Lesley, I think I killed him. What am

I going to do?"

"How did you do that?" Lesley was fast returning to her normal self. "We need to get out of here. Tell somebody about this. What did you kill him with?"

"Let's just go back. I've had enough." Gail leaned wearily against a rock. She remembered her friend's project and the reason for this trek and said, "Do you think there's a tree in back of the library that could symbolize such evil?"

Lesley didn't know if Gail meant the dead man on the ledge or her own actions.

~~~~~

About the only truth in this story is the mountain and the building of the freeway. Such enormous structures erected in the wilderness are both convenient and disturbing. The girls echo many college friends. The deranged man—who knows?

~~~~~

no good wind

blowin'   blowin' down, way down on Little Black Slough   no way outta' this one is there Baby Doll?   no way to fix it   no way to make it right   solve the problem
complete the square   square the circle   sing the song   ring the bells
no way   no way   no way   no way outta' this mess

I remember your fine blond hair blowin' in the wind, so fine, so fine
fine blond hair curling 'round that pretty skull of yours curling and blowin' and me a running from the wind running in my big ol' split out hikin' shoes hikin' down this empty highway an empty highway takin' me far away from you
and you a layin' in the water with your fine hair curling in the spreading ripples
the spreading ripples kissin' your nose, your teeth, your tiny ears
ripples of fear punching me to run faster

faster and faster and faster the ripples of fear hound me down the empty highway
in the dark dark night black jacket dark pants dark

hair dark skin dark   dark   dark soul

      I'm a shadow on the face of the earth an evil shadow a contemptible shadow

     a stinkin' running shadow down the center line of this highway down the center line of death

                       of death   death

  death blows in the south wind and the south wind blows me stinkin' and running away   from you you with your fine hair spreading ripples in the water

        tiny scum things goin' in and out of your tiny ears

             wind   wind?   blow me away like a dry leaf

                blow me to peace to safety

              blow my memory clean of you

           blot my soul of this scab

       scrub me clean turn back time

  but no, I hike the highway miles and miles and   miles till my knees shake and my chest feels like water and my stomach   cramps

   with fear and hunger

       and sorrow and the wind blows hard

         and cold

        the wind blows faint sounds

    to my waiting ears

         sounds of fear sounds of wailing

               sirens and engines

     wind you betray me

      wind you're blowin' me no good

              kill me wind   freeze me wind

         wind you're blowin' me no good

              no good no good

Back In Time: The Old Country

The Christmas Goat

Klara pulled the wool coat tighter around her shoulders. Its deep hood shielded her face from the sting of wind-driven snow until she turned to the north, but her old boots were hardly adequate protection against the wet and cold. She paced the narrow track from the farmyard to the main road, back and forth, stomping her feet and swinging her arms to keep warm. Her brother, Ivar, and sister, Stina, were late coming home from the neighboring farm. Fear that the two would miss the turn off from the main road had prompted Klara into the storm to watch for them. The snow now filled her tracks almost before she turned around at the corner of the barn.

It was the shortest day of the year and the thin gray daylight faded quickly. With the wind howling in her face Klara struggled towards the road again. She scrubbed a mittened hand across her face to clear her vision, then stood quiet beside the tall pine at the roadside and watched.

Look at the snow so beautiful against the dark

trees, so beautiful and so bitter. She ventured as far as the house-sized rock marking the overgrown path through the woods. She knew this was as far as she dared go. If she lost her sense of direction now, she would never find her way home.

Klara touched the rough surface of the stone, leaned into it for protection from the stinging snow. Her back to the rock, Klara peered intently into the blowing whiteness. She could make out several mounds of snow among the trees, but the path became invisible after a few feet. Were those mounds moving closer, she wondered? They grew darker against the snow, developed flapping appendages, which she recognized as beating arms, flowing scarves, pumping legs. "Ivar, Stina." Tears of relief crusted her cheeks as she threw her arms around her brother and sister. "This way. You're almost home."

With a great deal of shouting, stomping of snow rimed boots, and shaking of coats and mittens Ivar, Stina, and Klara ducked through the door into the warm front room of the house. The heat from the open fire folded around them and the heavy aroma of yellow pea soup and salt pork filled the air. A garland of lingonberry and pine branches on the door announced it was Christmas. Bleary-eyed, Klara thought the colors swirled brighter than she had ever remembered. The firelight, the candles, and the old lantern on the table alternately flared and flickered with the draft from the opened door.

Klara realized her father had been about to come looking for them. The ready lantern, the boots beside his chair, and the anxious look on his usually placid face told the story.

A noise drew her gaze to her mother, Anna, who stood in the shadows on the other side of the fireplace. A niggle of apprehension clawed at the back of Klara's throat when she saw her mother clenching and kneading a linen napkin between her hands. One of the good napkins passed down from a great-grandmother, thought Klara. Her mother's rough hands had worried the careful weave and picked at the delicate embroidery until it was frayed.

"Mamma was worried about you," said her father. "Wanted me to get the team out to look for you."

"Sorry, Pappa," said Ivar. "We had a late start, so we took the short cut and missed the path. If Klara hadn't spied us through the trees and hailed us, we'd still be walking."

Klara removed her coat and crossed the room. She tried to take the crumpled napkin from her mother, but Anna jerked back, turned away. "Mamma, Mamma, it's all right. Everyone is safe." Anna looked down at the ruined napkin in her hands and seemed to see it for the first time. With a gasp she threw it into the fire, then, as if nothing had happened, took Klara's coat and spread it on the drying rack beside the stove.

Anna gathered the other wet coats and scarves

near the stove. Her fingers smoothed and straightened the woolen material as she draped the coats over the drying rack. When blasting heat from the fire licked at the wet wool, a damp animal stink filled the room. Finished with the coats, Anna turned and looked at Stina. "Are you all right?"

"I'm fine, Mamma." Stina sat down to take off her wet boots. Her pale hair had come unpinned and fell forward over her face as she bent to unlace her boots.

Serious conversation came to an abrupt end with the appearance of the younger boys, Will and James. They were arguing and punching each other as they burst through the doorway, flushed and sweaty. Though close in age, the two boys were developing in different directions. Nine-year old James, with a stubborn concern for right and wrong in other people's lives, had little sense of his own flaws and thought he was being picked on by everyone. Will, on the other hand, was easy going, quick to laugh, and delighted in games, practical jokes, and tormenting James.

"What are you two into, now?" said Ivar. "Come tell me all about it."

The pair ignored Ivar and stood facing their father. "Will said that the *Jultomten* comes with presents on Christmas Day." James stood with his feet apart, his fists on his hips. "He'll go to Hell for lying. Make him stop."

"He'll come, I know the *Jultomten* will come." Will held his ground before James's moral pronouncement, but unshed tears made his eyes bright. "He's got to bring presents this year."

"Who is this *Jultomten*? A Christmas elf, perhaps." Mr. Larsson put aside the strip of leather he had been working with an awl and hammer. A neat row of holes already lined one edge of the strip. "I know the *Tomtens* are invisible little fellows who guard the farm. Your mamma leaves them a bowl of oat porridge on Christmas night."

James argued with his father. "That's superstition. The preacher said it was a sin to believe in the forest spirits."

Ivar tried to soothe young James who looked as if he was about to explode with righteous indignation. "Don't be so hard on him, James. It's only a harmless tradition."

James seemed not to hear and repeated his opinion. "It's wrong. It's a sin to tell lies."

Ivar tried another tack. "Everybody knows the Christmas goat brings the presents, but if Will wants to call him the *Jultomten*, what can it matter?"

"The Christmas goat never comes here, but I'll bet the *Jultomten* will come," said Will. He turned to James and grabbed him by the shirt front. "Did the goat ever bring you anything?"

Ivar gave up and turned to his father. "Will must have overheard the school teacher talking. He was all excited about a new fad in Stockholm. The German tradition of St. Nicholas as the bringer of Christmas presents is becoming very popular in the city, only they call him, *Jultomten*, the Christmas spirit. It's just a man dressed in a long red robe."

Stina interrupted, "I expect the old Christmas goat will keep on making his rounds of farm houses. We don't get much from him and we don't expect much."

James refused to give up. "It's all lies. Why won't you listen?"

Ivar interrupted, "He'll come this year, whatever you want to call him. I'm sure of it."

"How can an old straw goat bring presents? He isn't even alive." James was at odds with everyone now.

Tired of the argument, Will dropped his chin to his chest, laid his hands alongside his head like horns, and stomped his feet. When James ignored this mocking, he lunged at him with a bellow.

"Stop it. Nobody will come if you boys keep fighting and the snow keeps coming down." Mr. Larsson separated the two boys. "Go wash up for supper."

"You never know about these goats and elves. This may be the year they decide to stop here." Ivar grinned at Stina and she giggled.

Anna leaned over the iron pot hanging in the open fire, large wooden spoon in hand. "The soup is ready. Klara, help me dish up."

Thursday pea soup was a tradition dating back to before the Reformation, when the entire country observed Catholic fast days and feast days with a rigor worthy of Saint Peter, himself. The medieval Christmas fast had been a meatless fortnight before the season of over-eating that surrounded December 25th. Now it was merely the habit of yellow pea soup on Thursdays.

Ivar sat down next to his father and pulled his bowl closer. "Do you think there's a chance we can go to Christmas service at Smedjebacken this year?"

The Christmas service, the *Julotta*, was always scheduled to conclude with the sunrise. The sleepy congregation would stand and sing their alleluias to the accompaniment of the rising sun. Christmas celebrated the birth of the Son, but it also celebrated the rebirth of the sun.

Stina interrupted, "That would be fun. Could we, Pappa?"

Mr. Larsson seemed to give the question a good mulling over before he answered. "If the snow stops in the next day or so, we might consider it. The wagon has the runners on and the horses are in pretty good shape. Ten miles over packed snow would be fairly easy. Better than trying to get there through the mud."

Later in the evening, Klara surprised Ivar and Stina whispering together. When she asked, they told her they were talking about a school assignment. A bit of determined teasing failed to pry out their secrets, so Klara left them to their plotting. She had secrets of her own this year.

Too warm, now, Klara sat heavy-eyed by the fire thinking about her own Christmas surprise and wondered if this winter could possibly be as bad as predicted. This was the longest night of the year, the winter solstice. Tomorrow the sun would stay above the horizon an instant longer.

Klara thought back to the week before, when a tradition dating into the dim past was celebrated. Under the mistaken notion that December 13th was the longest day of the year, people gathered to call for the return of the sun, to celebrate a festival of light called St. Lucia's Day. Days of growing darkness stirred a primitive longing for the light, a longing born of fear and depression.

The Larsson's celebration of St. Lucia's Day had been minimal this year. It had been Stina's turn to play the part of St. Lucia, but she was away at school. That left Klara and the two little boys. Still, Klara decided she must make some effort to mark the holiday. She had climbed out of bed before the rest of the family. To stop her shivering she wrapped her outdoor cloak around her shoulders and poked up the embers in the fireplace. As the fire took hold, Klara put water on to boil for coffee. On the painted tin tray she assembled spoons, cups, and napkins. She added a plate of *tinbrod*, thin bread, a little butter and a piece of hard cheese. She robbed her mother's hidden cache of loaf sugar and added a few of the precious lumps. By then the coffee aroma had permeated the house and she could hear the rest of the family stirring. She slipped off her coat and carried the tray to her parent's bedside, humming a little of the Sankta Lucia song.

"Good morning, Pappa, Mamma. I've come to dispel the curse of winter darkness. Well, at least I've come with breakfast."

"What? No candles in your hair? No long white robe?"

"Sorry, Pappa. I'm just a stand-in Lucia. Maybe Stina will give you full measure next year." Klara smiled at the thought of Stina all grown-up and appearing in the morning darkness with candles in her hair, white gown graceful to the floor.

Anna frowned as she accepted the cup of coffee from Klara. "You used the store-bought coffee?"

Klara felt a twinge of guilt. She knew her mother had been brewing a mixture of roast grain to conserve the meager supply of coffee. "You deserve a good cup of coffee, Mamma, especially on Saint Lucia's Day."

The coffee reminded her of the meager supplies laid in for the rest of the year. Though several storms had battered them already, winter was only just beginning. The hens would not lay without the sun; the cow was almost dry; her father would have no work at the mines until spring thaw.

Unable to sleep, Klara slipped out of bed to wrap her Christmas gifts bought with her small cache of egg money. From her sewing bag she selected some pretty scraps of material. For Stina she had a hair brush and new ribbons, for Ivar a comb case with a mirror. She fervently hoped it would not embarrass him. James would get the paint set with its papers of dry pigment waiting to be mixed with linseed oil, egg yolk, or plain water. For Will there was the harmonica. Her parents would have coffee and a sack of hard candy they would undoubtedly pass out to the children.

On impulse she went to the shelf above the stove and brought down the family treasure, an antique chocolate set handed down from a great grandmother. She polished the dainty cups and placed one at each place at the table. Even the youngest children were given a sip or two of coffee on special occasions.

I can serve the coffee from the chocolate pot, she thought. By then it will be too late for Mamma to forbid it. She covered the readied table with a white cloth, hiding the gleaming cups from view. Then she piled the wrapped presents at the end nearest the window and went back to bed. This year the Christmas goat would visit the Larsson homestead.

Back In Time: The New Land

A BAD, BAD LAND

As I sit here in the dock awaiting trial, you may be wondering how a woman could get herself in this predicament. A newspaper crumpled on a bench catches my eye. I wish I could reach it, read it. They don't let me have the paper in jail. It's the Rapid City Journal with a headline about the Titanic sinking with many lives lost. I wonder if the paper mentions me, Carolina Bjorg, on trial for murder and about to lose her life. Very few females have been charged with murder here in the Dakotas and none has ever come to trial. It all started with Joe, but I should tell you a little about myself first.

I was born in Sioux Falls, ninth in a family of ten children. Nine girls and one lone boy. I was born after a gap of seven years, a rather nasty surprise for my poor mother no doubt, as was my brother, Jed, who came along the following year. Still, we were the babies of the family, petted and cooed over, played with, lugged around, doted on by our older sisters. And do I see even one of those fawning, kissy sisters here today as I scan the audience in the courtroom. No, of course not.

We were considered well off. Father worked at the bank; our two-story white house had indoor plumbing, electric lights, and a coal furnace. Mother had a girl to help in the kitchen and another woman came in for the heavy work, cleaning and laundry and such, once a week. My sisters had a tutor for the finer things not taught in the public school, needlework, manners, French conversation. They even had tennis lessons one year. By the time Jed and I were old enough to participate in this good life, it was gone, over and done with. Father suffered a re-occurrence of an old lung ailment and was forced into retirement. As his health declined, my sisters took turns nursing him and helping with the household chores. As soon as they were able, they escaped into marriage until only Jed and I remained. When Katie, sister number eight, married an Indiana farmer and left home, I was ten and Jed was barely nine. After the excitement of the wedding week, the flurry of cleaning, cooking, packing, parties, the ceremony, itself, seemed a solemn post script. I remember wandering through the silent house when Mother and I came back from seeing Katie and her new husband off at the railway station. We had left Jed to keep Father company since he was unable to leave the house by then. I asked Mother about Katie's room. Did she want it for a sewing room, should I dust and air it, move the lighter bits of furniture to the attic. She shrugged and told me to do whatever I thought best, so I pulled the shades and closed the door. Her and

Father's world was shrinking to a nub just as I was seeking wider horizons.

With Katie gone her sick room duties passed to me. We still had a hired girl, but she was a surly, lazy thing with an overwhelming fear of illness. She refused to carry anything into Father's room or touch his dirty dishes and linens. Help was hard to get at the wage Mother was willing or able to pay, so I did all of his washing up and laundry. The girl, I think her name was Tillie, did help me with ironing. A good thing, because I was too small and inexperienced to meet Father's high standards.

I learned a great deal at these weekly ironings with Tillie. While I kept the fire up and carried the hot irons to her, Tillie talked. She filled my head with tales of swamp creatures, hauntings, miraculous cures, potions and remedies for all manner of problem. Strange as it may sound, I actually found myself thumbing through these memories when things went awry in my isolated soddy on the lip of the Badlands. Like the time my second born, Emmy, got snake bit. Joe worked on the railway that summer so we saw him but seldom. The nearest doctor was at Wall, a hard half day's ride. I was so far gone with my fourth baby, I was afraid to attempt the ride on the rib-thin mustang that was supposed to be my transportation. Tillie had told me endless stories about snake bite from her early life in the bayous of Louisiana, but I knew the concoction of snake root and kerosene she claimed as a cure wasn't available to me. Desperate I substituted a poultice of sorrel leaves and vinegar. I had the dried herb on hand because it was commonly used to treat worms and stomach ache. Poor Emmy. Her little foot and leg swelled up huge. She screamed all afternoon; nothing I did could quiet her. Exhausted, she fell into a stupor near sundown. I cut slits in her skin to let the poison out and applied more sorrel. Wet rags were the only thing I had to assuage her fever. How I wished for ice, a doctor, someone to comfort the other children. I couldn't leave Emmy's side, so I gave Will and baby Nance dry bread for their supper and allowed them to take the yellow dog to bed with them. By God's grace Emmy survived, though her recovery was slow and her leg remained stiff and misshapen. When Joe came home, all he could do was yell at me for not salvaging the snake skin. He said it was worth a dollar stretched and dried.

I wonder why Emmy lived when it was so obvious death was at hand and, yet, Will died without an instant of warning. With Emmy I knew her time had come. I had hours to prepare myself, to imagine life without her bright smile and endless questions, to be sure I had done everything humanly possible to save her, to bid her farewell and Godspeed. But Will, dear son, my first born, always into mischief, strong and quick like his father. One second he is alive and racing to tell me about his coyote pup, the next he is stone cold dead. A burst blood vessel in his brain the doctor said later, nothing could have saved him. No time to prepare, no time for good-byes. I wish I had known then what caused Will's death. Joe blamed me and I blamed him. I wish it had been me instead.

Will was his father's son. I stress that because he was, indeed, Joe's child. He looked like him, walked like him, talked like him, but Joe just couldn't see it. I think it was this sneaking doubt that made the bond between us tear and grow to a huge chasm. Because Will was conceived before we moved to the wasteland, Joe had plenty of men to nominate to the position of Will's father. Each time he thought of another possibility, I suffered a period of his silent, brooding punishment. Each time I would rack my brain to remember the details of my conduct with Joe's accused and each time I found myself innocent of wrong doing. I would scream my anger silently and pound my fists into the mound of bread dough on the kneading board. Sometimes my tears dampened the leavened mass until I had to add more flour. How could you do this to me, Joe. Dear God, it hurts as if it happened yesterday. I glance down and realize I have gripped the rail of the prisoner's box so hard my knuckles are white. My hands ache when I release my grip.

Rubbing my swollen joints, I think about the long days of cutting sod for our house. Married barely a year, I worked alongside Joe, matching him block on block, wrestling the fifty pound squares of earth and prairie roots to form the walls of our home. At sundown I would stop work to gather dry grass and buffalo chips for our supper fire, while Joe cut a few more blocks. Early on I argued for a cold supper, but Joe had to have his coffee and it seemed a shame to waste the fire. We had brought bundles of fire wood along on the immigrant train. It was a precious commodity I worked hard to stretch. Whenever I trekked up the gulch for necessary business, I carried a basket to collect bits of dry grass, greasewood, Russian thistle, anything that might burn. It all came to naught the day some of Joe's old cronies arrived on their way to a new claim over on Cedar creek. They spent the night sitting around the fire, talking and drinking the whisky they had in ample supply. Joe used up most of our precious wood that night. He said, he cut it and he'd burn it if he felt like it. I crawled into my roll of blankets and cried myself to sleep.

When I married Joe, we planned to live with his parents and help work the family farm. My father had died, Jed had married and brought his bride, Lucille, home. She was a sweet girl, but her slovenly ways repulsed me. She often slept until noon, then expected me to fix her breakfast. Either Mother or I had to tidy her room and take care of her laundry. As the year wore on I realized I was little more than an unpaid servant and the work load could do nothing but grow. Mother was slipping, becoming more and more forgetful; Lucille was pregnant, and, worst of all, from my perspective, Jed had bought his wife a lap dog for her birthday. You wouldn't think a little dog could be much trouble, but this one refused to be house broken; it howled at night and chewed the drapes and chair legs. No matter how much Lucille fussed over it, the tiny beast continued to make us miserable. When it wasn't tearing at someone's shoe or sweater, it was nipping our heels or pulling the clean sheets from the clothes line. One of us would have to go and it sure didn't look like Lucille and the lap dog were going anywhere soon.

Compared to this chaos, Joe's family home seemed quiet, orderly, clean. Too clean and orderly, it turned out. During our courting time, I failed to notice the iron rule exercised by Joe's mother. Married, I found we were to leave our shoes at the side door before entering the house (the front door was reserved for the clergy and other important folk). Verbal tip-toeing was practiced when we were within her earshot. Serious conversation, jokes, and teasing was saved for the barn. In the eight months I lived there, I entered the dining room only to mop and dust. I glimpsed the interior of the parlor just once. My mother-in-law trusted its dusting to no one. Though Joe and I were given one of the larger guest rooms for our own, Joe wouldn't even touch me there. If it weren't for occasional romps in the hay barn at midnight, I'd have thought I had entered a nunnery.

It wasn't long before Joe was thinking about us heading out on our own. He brought home all sorts of money making schemes. Everything from selling tonic door-to-door, to going to Australia as sheep ranchers. The trouble with all of his ideas was money or, rather, the lack of it. His father told him he could expect no help from him. The farm was good enough for him and his grandparents before him, it should be good enough for us. We had managed to acquire about three hundred dollars, more than half from my brother, Jed, when some distant cousins came through on their way to claim free land in the western part of the state. They had maps, government pamphlets, and new dreams. Joe asked them a hundred questions, but hardly sat still long enough to hear the answers.

The idea of free land, a place of our own, was like a song in the morning. I caught myself smiling at odd moments, flicking dish suds at Joe when he walked through the kitchen, and dancing with my apron at the clothesline. Joe's mother was sure I was possessed by the devil and now I have come to agree with her. How easy it was to pick up that ax. Though I can only glimpse it sitting there on the evidence table, I can still feel the slight curve of its handle, the balanced weight of its steel head. It is a single bit ax, one edge honed sharp, the other a worn hammer head, one of the tools we bought just before we boarded the train.

We were to travel across the state in an immigrant train, the railroad's contribution to the settlement of the last best west. It was a romantic name for a common freight car. The day before departure we gathered our belongings on the siding, ready to load. We started with the old buggy Joe had bought from the local livery stable. I had argued in favor of buying a wagon with side boards, useful for hauling lumber and supplies, but Joe wanted something more stylish, more sporty. Next we loaded his riding horse who had proved himself to be both capable and willing to work in harness, a milk cow big with calf, several crates of chickens, and Barney, our yellow dog pup. We also had an iron stove, a kerosene lantern, a small table, rolls of rope, bundles of quilts, a ground tarp, hay for the animals, hoes, saws, a Dutch oven, and a few dishes. I had expected to ride in the regular passenger car with the other women, but Joe insisted I keep him company in the box car with our house plunder. He said it would be great fun sleeping in the hay, watching the scenery roll by the open door; it would be a camping trip, one last vacation before we got down to the work of homesteading, so we bedded down in the hay to wait for the early morning departure.

At the last minute Jed drove up in a livery wagon with Mother's oak rocking chair in back. She was certain I would need it when the babies started coming. I nearly cried when Joe lifted the fine old chair into the box car and pushed it roughly across the uneven floor to a spot beside the stacked hay.

By the time we reached Murdo I expect he had changed his mind about me riding with him. Holding a woman while she pukes out the open door of a box car rumbling across the prairie can do that to a man. I felt sorry for Joe, but in the long run it was his own fault. Weak with relief, I jumped out when the train stopped a short distance from the Murdo station to await shuttling onto a siding. We had been on the move for some twelve hours.

Government regulations dictated that the livestock had to be unloaded, fed and watered before we could continue on our journey, so we were stuck in Murdo for the night. After the animals were cared for, we tied the dog nearby and walked to the Murdo Hotel. We took supper and a room for the night, though Joe insisted we could sleep in the box car again. As it turned out Joe had little need for a bed. While I slept like the dead between dingy hotel sheets, he found a poker game where he managed to win eighteen dollars before he passed out. His friends carried him upstairs and left him in the hallway where I found him snoring the next morning. I helped him into bed, helped myself to a share of his winnings, and went down to breakfast, a twenty-five cent splurge for the Traveler's Special.

The rest of the train trip was slower because of the many stops at points closest to individual claims. Each time the train screeched to a stop we would climb down from our box car to stand in the gravel, peering up and down the track to see who was unloading for the trek across the plain. Between stops I sat in the rocker and enjoyed the scenery gliding by. Poor Joe, who wasn't used to strong liqueur, had a terrible whiskey hangover. When the train reached top speed, he would lay on the floor with his head out the door, gagging and hiccupping with dry heaves.

As morning passed into afternoon, I began to realize the isolation of our new home. Ours was the very last stop on the homestead trail. Another couple unloaded at the same time. They would travel with us for an hour or more, but then they would turn west to travel several more hours into the depths of the badlands. Without the benefit of the regular ramps and chutes of a rail yard, unloading heavy goods and livestock was difficult. But working in concert with the other couple and railroad employees anxious to move on, we managed to unload everything. Joe and I had a huge fight because our goods would not fit into the high topped buggy. No matter how we arranged and rearranged things, something had to be left behind and, of course Joe insisted on leaving the rocking chair and the box of house plunder. I argued for leaving the firewood and the glass paned windows intended for our new house. The weather would have little effect on them and we could drive back for them in a day or so. In the end our battle was a vain one. We left rocking chair, firewood, windows, the sheet iron stove, and the heavier tools. I tried hard not to cry as we drove off, but even Joe noticed and offered me his handkerchief. He said not to worry, he'd drive back in the morning to get the rest of our things. He could be awfully sweet at times.

We made quite a cavalcade winding through the huge piles of Russian thistle searching out a reasonably level path to our home sites. The McClearys, the family we were to travel with on the first part of our overland trek, led the way. They had a cutter and a freight wagon, both loaded to capacity with chairs, lumber, tools, and children. Two milk cows, three riding horses, and a number of goats were tied behind. Crates of chickens, ducks, and even a few turkeys were lashed in back of the house goods. A small organ with its carved stool had been lovingly stowed just behind the driver's seat in the big wagon. I knew the barrels and boxes held linens and china because Mrs. McCleary had told me all about each item. She said they had homesteaded before, before the six children had been born, and she had been so terribly unhappy in the bare cabin built by her husband and brother. She vowed she would never again be without her precious things, so when her husband decided to move farther west, she insisted on bringing all her pretties, pretties that had been in storage at her sister's house in Mason City all these years.

I envied her fine belongings, but they certainly slowed us down. Each hill, each dry wash, had to be inspected to see if the heavy wagon could safely cross without undue bumping. Several times fragile items had to be unloaded and hand carried over a particularly rough place. It was with regret, but also with relief we finally parted company a few hours later. We could move faster, but the silence of the prairie soon closed around us. I think Joe even felt it because he started singing all the silly songs we had learned as children.

When we reached Peach Creek, the singing stopped. We had missed the ford. Joe admitted he had no idea if we were above or below the ford, so we decided to cross where we were. The near bank was steep and muddy from the spring rains. The horse was tired, not used to pulling the heavy buggy over such rough ground. He balked when urged to move forward, so we climbed out and tried to lead him. Joe hit him a couple of hard licks with the whip, but the horse threw up his head and planted his hooves more firmly on the bank. In the end we unhitched the poor animal and led him across the creek. It wasn't hard to understand his reluctance when we reached the far bank weighted down with sticky mud. We wiped him down the best we could and tied him to a low hanging branch to wait. It took Joe and me several hours to unload the buggy and carry the stuff across. The buggy itself was another matter. Joe finally shucked off his mud-stiff pants and rode the horse back across the creek, hitched him to the empty buggy, and rode back, buggy lurching behind.

My first sight of our homestead was a real let down after the mess and worry of fording Peach Creek. We had bought an existing claim instead of starting from scratch. Joe had inspected it a few months ago, before the fierce spring rains. The corners were marked with rock piles and the outlines of a small sod building were visible. Lacking a roof, it had mostly washed away in the rains. I had been promised a tar paper shack, too, but no trace of it was visible. Apparently it had been scavenged for material by other settlers or, perhaps, the local Indians. I climbed down from the buggy and stared at my new home. Maybe it would look better in daylight, I thought. Right now the problem was supper and a place to sleep.

While Joe unhitched, I found the crude remains of a fire pit, cleared away the dry weeds, and started water to heating. I had salvaged the enamel coffee pot and iron skillet from the box of house goods we left on the siding, so I had coffee ready for Joe when he finished scraping mud clods from the animals and himself. We made do with bread and jam for supper. Washing up would have to wait until daylight because we had used all the water we had carried from the creek. Joe promised he would haul us some water from Wall when he went back for the goods we had left behind. Apparently Wall was the nearest town, though Joe was unsure of the distance because he had not been there before.

It was full dark by the time we were ready to sleep. Joe said it was no use to light the oil lamp, so we fumbled around in the dark until we found a smooth place to sleep. I shucked off my muddy skirt and shoes and rolled myself in a quilt. When I awoke just before dawn, a thin crust of frost covered everything. Frost in June, I should have known it was a portent of trouble. I pulled the quilt over my head and burrowed closer to Joe.

I shiver and pull my sweater closer around my shoulders. Most of the observers in the court room are wearing their coats and the jurors have the benefit of the wood heater on the far side of the courtroom. The judge has his robe and the lawyers are never still long enough to feel the January chill. Only the poor woman transcribing the proceedings seems as cold as I am. How can she sit there day after day writing down the horrible things being said. Her expression never changes, even when she records the depth and location of the twelve ax wounds they found on Joe's head and body. You wonder how things could have come to this. Maybe it had something to do with waiting.

I got an early start on waiting that first day on our new homestead. We got up as soon as the first light dribbled over the horizon. Joe wrapped himself in the still warm quilts and sat leaning against the buggy wheel. He wanted his coffee and a hot breakfast. Under the pretext of hunting some firewood, I made a flying trip up the nearest gully to attend to personal business. I was shaking with cold by the time I got back to camp with an armload of sticks. By the time Joe finished his coffee and pancakes he was bubbling with plans to drive to Wall, buy a water tank, fresh supplies, and pick up our stuff on the way back. He insisted I make him a list of things we needed even though I didn't know what was available or how much it cost. I finally wrote down things like coffee, bread, eggs, and soap and he hitched up the horse and drove off through the wasteland in the general direction we had come the day before. He said he could find the ford from this side and he should be back by supper time.

The morning went quickly. In anticipation of Joe's return I unpacked and set up camp as best I could. I hung the quilts over a scrub oak to air, worked the drying mud from my skirt, tried to clean my poor shoes, scoured the frying pan. By noon I knew I had to water the animals. I was afraid to release the chickens from their crate so I took the coffee pot and walked the mile or so back to Peach Creek for water.

The yellow pup followed me, sometimes bumping against my legs, never ranging out of sight. The pancakes he had for breakfast didn't agree with him and he gagged and hacked up every few steps. At the creek he rolled in the mud and lapped up a stomach full of water, most of which he threw up on the way back to camp. I poured water into the fry pan and let the chickens out of the crate to drink and forage for bugs. The pup made a dive for the chickens and upset the water pan. After I tied up the pup, I led the cow to the creek. While she had her drink, I tried to wash the mud from my skirt and shoes and filled the coffee pot again. The mud, both dry and fresh, stuck like cement. I gave up and led the cow back to camp. For once I was glad to be alone because I wore only my chemise and petticoat. In camp I turned the cow loose to scrounge what little grass she could find. I hung my ruined clothes on a bush and rubbed my shoes with a bacon end.

Joe had spent an unreasonable chunk of our money on work clothes before we left Sioux Falls. Now I decided to try a pair of his overalls. Before the hour was out it was as if I had never worn anything else. With the money I had squirreled away in my sewing box I vowed to buy a pair of work boots at the next opportunity.

That resolve lifted my spirits and I spent the rest of the afternoon making our camp snug and comfortable. Though the coffee water was hot and the beans and bacon cooked, Joe did not show up for supper. Just after sunset I gave up, threw the ruined beans to the yellow pup, and crawled into my nest of quilts. I jerked awake at each new sound in the night, but none of them announced Joe's arrival. Just before dawn I fell into a deep sleep and did not stir until the cow's low moans penetrated my brain.

I finally realized she must be in trouble. Groggy, almost drunk with sleep, I tried to pull on my stiff shoes. My head ached, my mouth tasted bitter as a copper spoon, my stomach lurched. The yellow pup, growling and dragging the quilts through the dirt, knocked over the water I had carried in for morning washing and coffee. I finally hustled myself barefoot through the brush to the cow. She was standing at the bottom of a dry wash, her hind end wet with birthing water, the tiny hooves of her calf barely visible. I checked to be sure it was the back hooves and that they were pointing the right way indicating a normal delivery. I found a place to sit and wait and soon saw the real reason for the cow's anxiety. A half dozen coyotes appeared like silent shadows against the opposite side of the gully. They, too, were prepared to sit and wait.

The bone deep exhaustion I felt that morning lingers in my memory, as does the rage I felt each time I drove the predators away from the helpless cow. Their attack grew fiercer when the calf finally slipped from the birth canal and the cow turned to clean her newborn. She suddenly decided to include me with the predators and charged me when I got too close. This, of course, left her calf open to attack by the coyotes. We were all frantic by the time I heard Joe's voice above us. Down here I shouted, bring your rifle. In no time Joe had the coyotes on the run and we were able to herd the cow and calf back to the relative safety of the camp.

How strange it feels to be reliving these painful hours of the past while I sit in this bleak courtroom. You would have thought my attention would be riveted to each word spoken against me, each motion, each maneuver by the earnest young lawyer hired in my defense, yet I have heard nothing of the morning's proceedings. Instead I hear Joe telling me how silly I am to be afraid of a few mangy coyotes, laughing at my worry over his absence, jeering the sight of me in his overalls. I consoled myself knowing the cow had birthed a healthy bull calf and we would have a supply of fresh milk in a few days. I nearly forgot my worry over my precious rocking chair Joe was to retrieve from the railroad siding miles away. Of course he had forgotten it. By the time he finally hauled it home the sun had blistered and whitened its fine rubbed finish, loosened a spindle in the arm, and burned a hole of resentment towards Joe into my heart.

I always thought a fresh milk cow was better than a bar of gold. We soon had a good supply of fresh butter and soft cheese. The clabbered milk fed the chickens and the yellow pup. I begged Joe for a couple of piglets to fatten with the surplus. He said we had to wait until spring, but in the mean time we could build a pen next to the lean-to we had made for the cow. Water continued to be our big problem. Joe had hauled two barrels from Wall, along with a couple of pounds of coffee and a sack of course flour, but a barrel of water lasted less than a week in the dry season. Joe enjoyed his trips to town and I always thought that was the reason he never made much progress developing a better water system.

Most of that first summer was consumed with cutting sod for our house and hauling water. Between bouts of morning sickness I planted a scrap of garden, but blistering heat and lack of water soon withered the tender plants. I didn't get to town with Joe until the first hard frost. We needed tar paper for the roof and supplies for winter. I had gone barefoot all summer and needed shoes in the worst way. At first Joe was reluctant to let me come with him. He insisted he could get me the right size shoes, but I held out and in the end made my first trip to Wall.

Wall was a welcome, almost overwhelming experience. It made me realize I had not spoken to a single soul, other than Joe, for nearly four months. After we bought flour, sugar, coffee, corn meal, salt, a side of bacon, roofing nails, and tar paper, I left Joe to entertain himself at the saloon. I had shopping of my own to do. I bought work boots, lard oil, a red checked oil cloth for the table, and a new mixing bowl. Joe had ruined mine stirring up some gooey concoction for the horse's hooves. Baking powder, tea, a sack of English walnuts, a nickels worth of horehound candy, a length of cotton print for curtains, a length of flannel to sew into baby clothes, things I had been thinking about all summer filled my box. One last purchase was a pair of overalls of my own. Embarrassed, I waited until the store owner's wife was on duty behind the counter. She assured me that several homesteading women had bought jeans for themselves lately, then she suggested a pair of bib overalls might be more comfortable for a woman in my condition. Surprised that she had noticed my swelling belly, I bought an extra pair in a larger size for the months to come.

So went the days at our homestead on the South Dakota prairie, hard work, tedium, plain food, isolation, small accomplishments, small tragedies. No one thing to give a body cause to snap, to rage against the universe, regret the day of their birth, not until the babies came. Will was first, born that winter, all red and slippery, howling his protest against the icy blizzard pounding our poor soddy. Joe did his best to help, but the whole birthing process made its mark on him. He kept his distance from the children forever after, leading me to believe it good reason to send the men folk out to boil water when babies are birthed.

Will was followed by Nancy, then poor Emmy who got snake bit, and then, after a gap of five years, darling Jack was born. We still lived in that dirt soddy. Joe had cut a place in the south facing wall for one of those precious windows we had hauled from Sioux Falls; the other one still leaned against the pig pen wall making a warm place for the yellow dog on sunny days. The yellow pup we had carried from Sioux Falls was long dead, poisoned by the bait laid out by some rancher in his battle against the coyotes. This dog was from her second litter. I had kept my hidden stash of money from running out by selling eggs from my growing flock of chickens, but the yellow pups proved to be an even better money source. Dogs were scarce on the prairie in those early days.

Joe tried to farm our land that first spring. He borrowed a team and a breaking plow from a distant neighbor and went to work. The parcel of land broken by the previous homesteader had grown up in rank wheat grass, but yielded to the plow eventually. The unbroken land was a different matter. After two or three trips up and down the uneven field both Joe and the horses were shaking with exhaustion. So much for adding more tillable fields to the homestead.

We sowed the land to oats, watched the green blades flourish under the summer sun, until it was time for the grain to head out. With the moisture in the soil gone, buffeted by hot winds, the oats were soon on the verge of drying up. Desperate to save something, we cut the ten acres by hand and dried it for hay. A neighbor offered us six dollars for the entire crop if we would haul it to his barn and fork it into the loft. That figured out to sixty cents an acre. We kept our hay to feed the milk cow and her calf through the next winter.

Joe worked for various ranchers and neighbors to eke out enough money to get us through until another crop came to harvest. He picked corn for five cents a bushel, helped one man put up an earthen dam, another dig a well. For each job he was gone from home for a week or more, eating with the family who hired him, sleeping in their barns or sheep wagons. He admitted himself that he enjoyed the visiting immensely.

The first year's crop failure turned into a yearly event. We tried corn and had to cut it when the ears were short and milky to avoid total loss from powder black fungus. We fed it to the cow through the winter and in the spring she dropped a dead calf. Another year we planted milo and, like the oats, it flourished full and green, until the hot winds began to blow out of the badlands. I watched that green promise wither and die while I waited for Joe to return home. He had developed a bit of a reputation as a guide for the various people who showed up to see how folks lived on the prairie. A busy rancher or a hard working homesteader would send a buckboard or a spring wagon to fetch him and Joe would be off to show well-dressed easterners the strange formations of the badlands, the herds of antelope grazing the high plateau, the rustic towns of Wall and Wasta. Sometimes he was commissioned to take visitors as far as the Black Hills, a three or four day journey where the party would sleep in tents and eat around a cheery campfire. All provided by the rancher, of course. Joe was well fed, but seldom paid for his services. I argued, raged, and ranted at him about this, but he ignored me. It was all a great lark for him.

His guide work came to a halt several years when he took a job with the railroad. I saw him only a few days each month and when he was home he seemed like a different person. Loud, engrossed in repeating dirty jokes he had learned from his fellow railroaders, swigging from the flask of whiskey he carried everywhere, he frightened the children and had little to say to me except criticism. He was away working on the railroad when Emmy got snake bit and, again, when a month later, our fourth child was born. He did make it home a few days after Jack's birth. I felt huge relief. The chore of tending a new baby, worrying after Emmy's recovery, keeping the livestock fed and safe was compounded by prolonged drought and a curse of grasshoppers. Peach Creek was totally dry and the hoppers had stripped the oat fields bare.

Joe hauled water and talked about getting a well digger out from Rapid City. He played with baby Jack and taught Will some new knife tricks. Best of all, we talked and flirted like in the old days. I even found one of my old dresses and put my hair up for him. A few days later my relief turned to frustration and anger when I found that he had quit the railroad. He said the work was too hard, too boring, and besides, he had a new job. A rancher near Wasta was paying him to give the grand tour to visitors from Kansas City. If he had warned me, told me he was unhappy with his job, given some clue to his future plans, I might not have reacted as I did. Now two of the women in that party sit waiting to testify to my proclivity to violence. Look at them sitting there looking so modest in their long skirts and high collars, faces wiped clean of rouge. A careless onlooker might think them school marms, but I know them for the hussies they are.

Joe had been home less than a week when a great cloud of dust appeared on the horizon. As the dust trail came closer, I could see that it was a large wagon of some kind. By the time the four horse hitch crossed the shallow wash leading to our place it showed itself to be a handsome brougham coach. Even a layer of dust could not hide the polished mahogany body, the brass trim, the velvet side curtains. Joe barely had time to slick back his hair and grab his hat before the carriage drew up at our front door, trampling my poor struggling flowers and sending the chickens to roost in the sage brush. The lad at the reins apologized to Joe, saying he tried to convince the women folk to wait in the hotel at Wall while he came for him. Joe seemed confused, obviously furious with the driver, but wanting to be officious to the three women descending from the carriage. With a string of curses he sent the children into the house; he tried to bully me into retreating, but I stood numb and wooden, my mouth open with surprise and offense. With baby Jack at my breast I glared at the trio of women standing in my dooryard stomping dust from their dainty patent leather shoes. I became acutely aware of my own stringy hair and dirty overalls as I watched them remove their sweeping picture hats to better help each other pat and smooth already perfect hair-dos, shake out long flouncy dresses, and apply fresh lipstick to lips already crimson bright. I pulled Joe aside and asked him what sort of women could these be. He muttered something about them being entertainers and pulled away. Entertainers, my eye. This was a madam and her whores. I clutched the baby hard to my breast; he set up a terrific howling, but I ignored it in my frantic attempt to drag Joe away from these predators. He pushed me aside and escorted the women back to the carriage, apologizing about the lack of hospitality. I ran after them screaming, but baby Jack slowed me too much. Joe slammed the carriage door and jumped to the driver's seat to take the reins before I crossed the yard. I pounded on the mahogany side panel and barely had time to jump aside when Joe whipped the horses and turned the carriage around in the yard. I must have looked like a mad women standing in the road throwing clods of dirt at them, screaming, barely keeping hold of baby Jack, my hair whipping, tears running black rivers down my face. What good can they possibly testify about me.

Dazed, I crawled into bed and stayed there. Will, with little Nance, did his best to take care of the animals. Poor Emmy tried to feed the baby, but his screams discouraged her and she soon brought him back to me. When the bread and fat back ran out; when the children's efforts to rouse me to action failed, Will bridled Joe's saddle horse and made his way to the closest neighbors, some four miles away. I managed with

Emmy's help to wash myself and comb my hair before the Ericksons followed Will into the dooryard. I could tell Mrs. Erickson thought me a lazy slut, but she did her best to set things right. The smell, alone, nearly sent her reeling. Mr. Erickson left immediately to haul us some water and buy cornmeal and fatback. I felt some better by the time they completed their mercy mission, but I know it counted heavy against me when I begged Mrs. Erickson to take baby Jack with her. I was so afraid I would do the poor little thing mortal harm. She refused.

When Joe came home two days later, I made a great effort to be cordial and welcoming, determined to be the good wife, but he chattered endlessly about his latest adventure. Miss Bee thought he was so, so brave chasing away a thieving coyote. Miss Star hung on his every word. Madame Smith encouraged him to share their private stock of French wine each evening around the campfire. I gave up and retreated into black silence. Joe ate his supper of bread and clabbered milk, but talked endlessly about the superiority of Russian caviar, beefsteak grilled to brown perfection, crisp lettuce and tomatoes tossed together with a sauce both sweet and vinegar tart. Salad he called it.

I pushed my plate away and finished nursing baby Jack. Joe started another story, this one about Deadwood. I couldn't stand another word. I wrapped the baby in his worn thin, washed gray blanket and put him in Joe's arms. I made a futile attempt at wiping spit up from my shirt as I left the table. Where could I go to cry my bitter tears. The house, a bare twelve by twelve room, had no private place; the board privy fumed the eyes and turned the stomach; I ran across the yard to pour out my frustration in the cow shed.

Any hope I might have had that Joe would follow me with concern and apology to salve my wounded soul were dashed when I heard the splash of discarded wash water, followed by the crash of the bar across the door. Locked out of my own house, I made a nest in the hay and cried myself to sleep.

If Joe thought a night in exile would bring me to my senses, he was mistaken. Cold and stiff, I resolved to find a way out of this hell on earth. I fried bacon, mixed a batch of corn muffins, and opened a jar of wild berry jam. With the fresh milk and hot coffee it seemed a feast. Joe barely noticed. He talked about a coyote den he had spotted a mile or two up the Wasta road. Will was bright-eyed and red-cheeked with excitement. I worried some because he was wheezing, too, but, then, the fresh air would probably help. They cooked up an expedition to dig out a pup to raise. Joe had seen a tame coyote in Deadwood and felt it would be great fun to raise one. Maybe make good money with it, too. As soon as breakfast was over, they gathered ropes, burlap bags, heavy gloves, and rode off.

It was dark when they returned on foot. Joe led the way, carrying a coyote pup, trussed up and secured in a sack. Will walked behind leading the horses. Neither horse would tolerate the smell of coyote. Both Joe and Will seemed exhausted, but they worked past midnight making a pen they thought would hold the animal. When they dumped the pup out of the bag, it struggled so much they decided to leave it tied up until morning. At Will's tearful insistence, Joe untied its mouth so it could drink.

I was jarred awake at first light by shouting in the yard. I was surprised to find both Will and Joe were already up and out. By the time I finished dressing I could hear Joe swearing at Will, calling him stupid and babyish. When I appeared in the doorway, Joe ducked out of the low roofed shed with a handful of shredded rope in his hand. Will ran across the yard towards me. He never made it. He stopped half way and sort of twisted a little, his mouth open. Then his eyes clouded over and he dropped like a stone to the hard packed earth. A tiny thread of blood marred his face.

Dear God, how could this happen. Not even in my worst nightmare did I ever see myself kneeling in the dust holding my dead child, my firstborn. Am I so horrible, God. Can my sin be so great that you deal with me like Pharaoh, back there in Egypt. I barely remember what happened after that. Joe hitched up the buggy and took poor Will into town. Maybe he couldn't grasp what had happened, maybe he refused to believe our boy was dead. The funeral was a few days later. Will was buried in the cemetery at Wall, all alone. I don't know if the coyote pup was old enough to survive on its own. I found it dead in the brush a few days later. I mourned anew as Joe shoveled it into a shallow grave.

Back at the house Joe and I started ranting at each other. What had he been thinking, dragging that child along on his coyote hunt, keeping him up all hours, getting him over excited. Couldn't he see that Will was flushed, exhausted. Joe tried to distance himself by denying Will was his son, accusing me of unspeakable things. Attacked, my resolve crumbled. I turned my blame on myself. Why had I let Will go with Joe, why didn't I speak up when I saw his flushed face, his rapid breathing. Why didn't I take better care of him. Hold him, keep him from harm.

When Joe found he had the advantage, when he saw me turn the blame inward, he became aggressive. He stalked around the small room, a room made hot, oppressive by too much fire in the stove. He seemed to grow until he filled the whole house with his anger. When he reached out and grabbed me by the shirt front, I thought the Devil, himself, grappled me. I tried to shove him away, but he held tight and slapped me hard enough to snap my head back. Stop screaming, stop. I heard the words, but didn't know whose mouth screamed, whose demanded silence. Joe hit me again, with his fist this time. I slumped against him and he pushed me against the hot stove. Frantic to escape, strong with pain, I reached for a length of stove wood. My hand closed on the smooth, familiar ax handle instead. With the long ingrained motion of chopping wood, I arched my back and raised the ax over my head. The blade hit the low ceiling and bounded forward to strike Joe over the left ear. It was a glancing blow, but it dazed him. When he staggered out into the yard, I followed. He tripped and fell against the pen he had built for the coyote pup. I could stand it no more. I raised the ax again and again. Would his screams ever stop, I wondered, then I realized it was my voice. It rose to meet the screams of the children huddled in the doorway.

I stood frozen, still holding the ax. Why doesn't Will take the girls and the baby somewhere safe. Hours later the neighbors found me wandering in the sagebrush, holding the ax tight to my breast. When I asked about the children, they assured me they were fine. Fine? How could they be fine if Will was dead, I asked. Had I killed him, too. They looked at me and shook their heads. The sheriff came for me, then. Now I sit waiting for you to pass judgment on me, though there is little more you can take. Joe and Will are dead. I finally understand that. Emmy, Nance, and baby Jack have gone to live with Jed and Lucille, the livestock was auctioned months ago. Without heat and upkeep, the sod house will crumble into the dirt, the plowed fields will grow up in thistles, wind and rust will carry off the last of our few possessions. It will be as if we never lived. Can you pass a judgment worse than that?